"It's time w

Crackling with electricity, she averted her gaze. Afraid of...she didn't know what, but AJ made her uncomfortable. His confidence, his strength, his wealth intimidated her. Two people couldn't be more different. "But there's no one around to see us."

"If you can't be comfortable with me close to you, touching you, we'll never be able to pull this off with an audience." He stroked her skin, sending her pulse rate climbing. "Is this so bad?"

"No." Her hand snuggled against his, their fingers laced together in a natural way. Though she'd die before admitting that.

"If we're going to sell being a couple, there's something else we need to practice. Kissing in public."

Her heart slammed against her chest. "You want to kiss me now?"

"Holding hands worked. Kissing seems the next logical step."

AJ's lips touched hers. Soft. Warm. Yummy.

Remember, he's not your boyfriend.

But the truth was so easy to forget when the kiss felt this good.

Dear Reader,

I'm so excited to be a part of the Special Edition line and introduce you to the Cole family from Haley's Bay, Washington. The town was dreamed up after my family stayed in a yurt at Cape Disappointment. A field trip to the Maritime Museum in Astoria, Oregon, led me to brainstorm a series set in the area. Fostering cats for a local no-kill animal shelter helped me develop my characters, billionaire AJ Cole, nanny Emma Markwell and a foster cat named Blossom.

My foster cats have all been seniors with medical issues, but I wanted Blossom to be younger so she could have a full and long life with her own happily-ever-after ending. I also decided she should be a diva cat.

Imagine my surprise when, after I sent off the first three chapters of this story, I picked up a fifteen-year-old cat to foster, and in a moment of life imitating art, discovered she shared a few not-so-nice characteristics with Blossom! Hissing, biting and scratching aside, my foster cat seemed so sad, wasn't eating and faced serious medical issues. She hated other animals (we have dogs and cats). She barely tolerated us.

Her month-long stay has turned into six months. She's doing so much better now and purrs when we pet her. Maybe she can give Blossom lessons. Even a diva kitty can soften the hardest of hearts. AJ Cole had better watch out!

I hope you enjoy visiting Haley's Bay!

Melissa

photographs she'd seen of AJ. Over six feet with a beard, he looked more like a conquering warrior than computer geek turned billionaire. Libby described her boss as gorgeous. The guy might be attractive with a hot body, but Emma had never been a fan of tall, dark and dangerous men with facial hair. "You call him Attila."

"Only when I'm hungry or PMSing or overworked."

Libby sounded exhausted. But recovering from emergency surgery while on a business trip to the East Coast would wear a person out. "So that leaves what? Two days a month?"

"Ha. Ha. AJ's a good boss who pays me extremely well."

"A good boss does not wake you up in the middle of the night to order flowers for his woman du jour. Or make you spend Christmas on an airplane instead of with your family. Or put his interview on CNBC ahead of your abdominal pains. All that money he pays you is worthless if you're dead."

"Hey, I'm very much alive."

No thanks to Mr. Atticus Jackson Cole. The what-ifs surrounding Libby's appendix turned Emma's stomach into enough knots to make a Boy Scout proud. "I'm thankful you're alive."

"I'm thankful you're filling in for me on such short notice." Libby, who focused on what her boss might need before he realized he needed something, didn't miss a beat. Even when connected to an IV and on painkillers. "Did you have a shot of tequila?"

"It's still morning."

"Remember what happened when we flew to Mexico?"

"Of course." Flying for the first time on a spring break trip to Puerto Vallarta had nearly turned into a one-way trip. Boarding a plane…no big deal. Accelerating along the runway…no big deal. Feeling weightless when the wheels lifted off the tarmac… Emma tapped her toe, a race-walk patter catching up to her marathon-run pulse. "Well, except for the flight home. You got me so drunk I passed out before the plane left the gate."

"I did that on purpose, and my plan worked. You didn't throw up. Go down a shot. For medicinal purposes. You need to settle your nerves for the flight."

Getting drunk at ten in the morning on the first day of a new job wasn't an option today. Emma would have to tough out the flight without alcohol. She'd survived worse, right? "My nerves are fine."

"Your voice sounds an octave higher."

"Bad connection."

"I hope so, because AJ's jet just landed."

The phone slid from Emma's sweat-slicked hand. She tightened her grip. "How do you know that?"

"I'm paid to know these things." Libby's words had a sharp edge, the way she sounded when handling a rare mishap. "But don't worry. The majority of your work will be party planning. But you might have to remind AJ that he's on vacation."

Libby's new tone and her old tales told Emma that caring for a dozen kids in training pants running with open pots of finger paints might be easier than assisting one billionaire while he tried to relax on a trip to his hometown. "I can't believe I'm going to be doing your job."

"You're perfect. You've dealt with angst-ridden teens, tweens with horrible attitudes, tantrum-throwing kindergartners, pampered preschoolers and toddlers with death wishes. You can handle anything, including AJ."

"I don't know about that." Emma watched a little girl carrying a stuffed dog and her mother talking into a cell phone walk into the restroom. "A bachelor billionaire with no kids doesn't need me."

"AJ needs you." Certainty filled Libby's voice. "Don't let his type A personality get to you. Billionaires aren't that different from toddlers except they know how to use silverware and occasional manners. Sometimes. Trust me, they need direction and supervision."

"You'd think he could pull together his grandmother's birthday party."

"AJ doesn't make his own dinner reservations," Libby said matter-of-factly. "Arranging his grandmother's soiree on his own is out of the question."

Emma's insides twisted. "Soiree sounds fancier than a party."

"Semantics. Stop worrying. You threw a spectacular birthday party for the twins."

Abbie and Annie. Cute six-year-old twins Emma had cared for the past year.

Trey Lundberg. Their handsome, widowed father who was about as perfect as a dad could be.

A weight pressed against Emma's chest. She'd stopped working for Trey three months ago. He'd made his personal interest in her clear and suggested they go out without the girls. Everything Emma wanted—a family of her own and the house with the white picket fence—had been within her grasp. But something had felt off. The idea of a ready-made family appealed to her, but Trey was still grieving the loss of his wife. Any feelings he had for Emma couldn't be real. Not that soon after burying the mother of his children. The more Emma had thought about going after her dreams with Trey, the more wrong doing so had felt. So she quit.

She shifted the phone to her other ear. "The twins were easy. They're little."

"AJ's grandmother is little. Barely five feet tall from what I've heard."

Emma sighed. "Libby."

"What? You have all the skills needed for my job. I could never do yours because of the crud and ick factor."

True. Libby didn't do crud or ick. She moved ten feet away from people who sneezed. She used two napkins during meals. She carried hand sanitizer at all times.

Emma never minded the messes kids made. Holding tissues during nose blowing. Wiping jelly spots off Abbie's cheeks. Helping Annie change her sheets before anyone noticed her wet bed.

A lump formed in Emma's throat, pressed upward. No regrets. She couldn't work for the Lundbergs when she didn't have the same feelings for Trey as he had for her. She'd helped find her replacement, trained the new nanny and told the girls to call if they needed anything…anytime.

A wistful, but not unexpected, sigh escaped. She wanted to find that special someone who would take care of her the way she took care of everybody else. Too bad happily-ever-after endings happened only in storybooks, not real life.

Emma cleared her throat. "The cruddy stuff isn't so bad. There's lots of fun to be had on the playground, believe it or not."

Except on the swings. She hated swings.

"I'll take your word for it," Libby said.

Emma's name sounded over the PA system. Every muscle group bunched, including ones she'd never met. Her stomach jangled, a mix of worry and trepidation.

She'd ridden enough elevators and carnival rides to know her tummy's reaction to weightlessness. Antigravity was her proven enemy, its falling sensation her greatest fear.

She blew out a puff of air. "Time to go."

"Good luck, not that you need it."

She swallowed. "Thanks."

"Have a good flight."

The line disconnected.

Emma tucked her phone into her tote bag, hand trembling. She swung the leather strap over her shoulder then picked up the cat carrier. "Here we go, Blossom."

The cat's snarl sounded like a combination of moan, hiss and spit. An omen of things to come? Emma hoped not.

The jet taxied on the tarmac in Hillsboro, Oregon. Except for a slight movement of AJ's tablet on the table in front of his seat and a glance out the window, he wouldn't have realized they'd landed. Not surprising. His flight crew consisted of top-notch, former military pilots. AJ never worried what was happening in the cockpit. But he was worried about the stranger, a nanny with a cat, who would be his assistant for the next five days. AJ rubbed his chin.

Emma is my best friend. She's smart and conscientious. A hard worker. She doesn't like to fly, but trust me. She's the perfect person, the only person, to take my place while you're in Haley's Bay.

Libby had been his personal assistant for two years. He had no reason to doubt her. Relying on her recommendation made more sense than yanking an employee away from other duties or hiring an untested temp from a service. A nanny should be able to follow directions, entertain his brother Ellis's kids at their grandmother's birthday party and, most importantly, deal with AJ's family. He wasn't a fan of cats, but he hoped the feline would be a distraction. The more attention his family gave the cat, the less they would give AJ. A win-win situation for all involved. Mostly him.

Dad wouldn't say much, if anything, unless forced to talk by Mom. The man would never forgive AJ for leaving Haley's Bay and the family business after graduating from college. The fact that he'd bailed out the fishing company during the economic downturn had only made his father resent AJ more. As if he'd had any other choice.

What was he supposed to do? See his family bankrupt and out of work, especially Ellis with a wife and two kids? No way. AJ had the means. Not helping would have been worse. Unthinkable.

He would never apologize to his father or anyone in his family for choosing to make billions with a computer instead of breaking his back working on a boat. AJ regretted nothing. He doubted his dad could say the same thing, if Jack Cole ever decided to talk to his oldest son again.

AJ wasn't sure how his four younger brothers would react to his being home. Only Grady, the youngest of the family, kept in touch. At least AJ wouldn't have to worry about the female members of the Cole family.

The Cole women would welcome him home with smiles and hugs. His grandmother, mom and two sisters called, texted, Skyped and visited him as much as they could. Though the four would likely be butting their noses into his life and asking much too personal questions while he was there. His stomach tightened.

Why had he wanted to come back? Oh, yeah. His grandmother's eightieth birthday.

An alarm sounded. The buzzing filled the cabin and made him glance at his tablet.

A message illuminated the screen. Conference Call—Marketing Department. Libby must have set his clock when he said goodbye at the hospital. The woman was the definition of *competent,* vital to his success for keeping his life running smoothly.

If only Libby were here with him. Damn appendix. Striking her down in New York. He balled his hands. AJ couldn't believe Libby had hidden her condition from him until it was almost too late. A foolish move, but one done out of loyalty to him. She knew how much he relied upon her. Or had until leaving him stuck with a nanny from Portland, Oregon.

If AJ didn't know better, he would think his father planned this. But nothing, not a hospitalized assistant or a cat-carrying nanny, would stop AJ from showing his family how far he'd come. Nothing was going to stop him from making a triumphant return to Haley's Bay.

Nothing at all.

Emma stepped outside the terminal, a sunny August sky overhead. Flying was safer during good weather, right?

But the roar of engines weighted her feet like chimney bricks.

For Libby. Step by dragged step, Emma crossed the tarmac toward a new-looking jet. Her heart pounded in her throat.

For Libby. Emma clasped the jet's railing. Her legs trembled—*don't stumble*—and she forced herself to climb the short staircase, one step, then another, followed by two more.

For Libby. Emma stepped into the plane. The hair on the back of her neck and arms prickled, ramrod straight beneath her sweater.

Noise from planes taking off and landing faded. Air-conditioning cooled her skin. The jet's interior muted tones exuded calm comfort. The plush carpet and cushioned chairs were a hundred and eighty degrees different from flying on a packed 737 with zero legroom and no empty seats. This time might be different.

"Welcome aboard, Miss Markwell." An attractive woman with long blond hair, a light blue blouse and navy slacks greeted her with a bright, white-tooth smile. "I'm Camille. I'll be your flight attendant today."

"Hi, I'm Emma." She forced a first impression smile and raised the cat carrier, welcoming the distraction. "Is there a place this should go?"

"I have the perfect spot." Camille took the carrier. "What's your cat's name?"

"Not my cat. She's a foster. Long story. But her name is Blossom. Thank you."

Camille peered into the carrier. "Hello, Blossom."

The cat's growl, a hair-raising, guttural sound, made Emma cringe.

Eyes wide, the flight attendant drew back. Her at-your-service smile faltered. She lifted the carrier away from her body as if radioactive waste filled the inside, then tipped her head to her left. "AJ's in the cabin."

"Thank you."

Emma passed between two forward-facing leather-covered captain's chairs. Each seat contained a television screen and game controller. The understated look was more luxurious man cave than flashy flaunt of wealth.

The next row faced backward. Someone with a head of thick brown hair occupied the seat to her left.

Attila. Atticus. AJ. This had to be him.

Libby thought the world of her boss, when she wasn't complaining about AJ. She described him as exacting. "Workaholic" was how Emma imagined him, based on how many hours he kept Libby working. And prompt. Libby said he would fire a manager if a project went over schedule, break up with a woman if she arrived late for a date and eviscerate a chef if forced to wait between courses.

Not everything Emma had heard about AJ Cole was awful. He paid employees well, was a philanthropist and doted on his grandmother, who visited him in Seattle at least once a month. The guy couldn't be all bad if he was throwing his grandma an eightieth birthday party—make that a soiree.

Voices sounded. Three or four.

Emma didn't see anyone else on board. She stepped closer.

The brown-haired man sat with a tablet in front of him. Three other faces appeared on the screen. One, a woman, spoke about branding.

Emma glanced from the tablet to her temporary boss. Whoa. A six-foot-plus mass of male hotness sat in the seat. A guy with no beard.

She blinked. Refocused. Still hot. Definitely AJ. She recognized his intense green eyes from the photographs.

Yum. Libby called her boss a nice piece of eye candy, but now that Emma was standing next to AJ Cole, he seemed more like a five-pound box of gourmet chocolates. Mouthwateringly delicious.

His gray suit jacket, expertly tailored, accentuated straight, wide shoulders. Unruly brown hair, curly at the ends, fringed the starched collar of his white dress shirt. His ruggedly handsome features fit perfectly together, making her heart accelerate like a car on a racetrack.

His smoldering gaze met hers.

Her throat tightened. She wished he hadn't shaved his beard so she wouldn't find him attractive. Then again, she still might. A photograph couldn't capture the 3-D version of the living, breathing man.

He motioned with his finger to the seat facing him. A small table separated the two chairs.

Emma removed the tote bag strap from her shoulder and sat. She ignored the conversation from the conference chat, not wanting to eavesdrop. She pressed each button to see what it did. Peering inside the pouch on the side of her seat, she saw a barf bag. She hoped she wouldn't need it.

The decibel level of the conference call rose. Voices talked over one another. Not quite a debate, but a lively discussion.

Her gaze fell on AJ's face. Talk about stunning. He laughed at a joke, softening the planes, angles and lines of his face. She focused on his mouth, zeroed in on his lips. Bet he was a good kisser.

What in the world was she doing? Thinking? AJ wasn't only her boss. He was also Libby's boss.

Emma looked at her lap. The seat belt ends lay on either side of her. She fastened the buckle and tightened the strap, as if the pressure could squeeze out her nonsensical thoughts before she embarrassed Libby and herself.

So what if the real-life AJ Cole was more attractive than his photographs? He was her boss, not a random guy she could flirt with at Starbucks then breeze out the door without a look back. Besides, he wasn't her type. She preferred a family man. Not a guy who, according to Libby, hadn't visited his family in ten years.

"Don't do that." AJ's hard tone made Emma jump. "If any of you disturb Libby while I'm away, you won't have a job when I return. Understood?"

Not so bad. Emma hadn't expected him to stick up for Libby.

"See you on Monday," he added.

The words *Don't bother me* were implied.

He tucked his tablet into the side pocket of his seat. "Emma Markwell."

His deep voice flowed through her veins like warm maple syrup. She fought the urge to melt into her seat. "Hello, Mr. Cole. It's nice to meet you."

His critical gaze ran the length of her, scrutinizing, as if she were a line of bad computer code wreaking havoc with his program. *This* was the man she expected minus the gorgeous face and athletic physique.

"Libby tells me you're a Martha Stewart–Mary Poppins mash-up, able to master home, hearth and heathen children."

"I don't have anything magical to pull out of my tote bag, but I do have a few modern-day equivalents for tricks and can spell supercalifragilisticexpialidocious backward." Something she'd learned being the nanny of a gifted child one summer.

"So you have no magic, but you brought a homeless cat."

His eyes were flat, no glint of humor or spark of amusement. Was this the intimidator Libby told Emma to ignore?

"Libby assured me that bringing Blossom was acceptable." Emma's voice sounded hoarse. She cleared her throat.

"If it was a problem I would have hired you a cat sitter." He shrugged off his suit jacket, tossed it onto the seat across the aisle, then buckled his seat belt. "My niece, nephew and cousins' children will play with the cat. Just keep the beast away from me."

"Allergic?"

"No."

Camille picked up the jacket, glanced at the seat belts fastened across their laps, then headed to the front of the jet.

The silence made Emma bristle, reminding her of the impending takeoff. She needed to distract herself. "Not a fan of cats?"

His lips narrowed, reducing their kissability factor by 70 percent. Not that she would ever kiss him.

"If you must know, they're pampered, vile creatures. I don't see the appeal."

His good looks had sparked an initial attraction, but his fire-extinguishing personality was making sure no flames erupted. She, as his employee, should let his words drop and discuss what her job responsibilities would be. But the cat lover in her couldn't do that. Nor could the friend in her, either. His lack of warmth and understanding he displayed with the cat probably also translated to his over-working Libby to the point of her almost dying.

"Blossom is not a pampered cat, Mr. Cole. Her owner died. The family didn't want to be bothered so surrendered the cat to an animal control facility in California. She ended up on a kill list. The shelter I volunteer for in Portland stepped in to rescue her. Blossom lived with thirty-five other cats until the space flooded yesterday. She had to come with me as a foster or spend the next week in a metal cage at a vet's office."

"Not pampered." He sounded more amused than irritated. "I stand corrected."

"Thank you for admitting that."

"I hear a 'but' coming."

Libby had said AJ didn't like being wrong. Emma didn't want to annoy him or upset him, but she had more to say. She scraped her teeth across her lower lip. "I've said too much."

"Perhaps, but I'd like to know."

Libby had told Emma to do what he requested without

asking too many questions. But this probably wasn't what her friend meant.

"Go on," he urged.

"Well…I'm sorry, but you're wrong about cats. They're intelligent, independent and inquisitive. They're amazing pets and have made innumerable people happier for their company."

His eyes widened, then narrowed. He pressed his steepled hands against his lips.

Uh-oh. He didn't seem to like her answer. "Remember, you wanted to know," she reminded.

"I did." He lowered his hands. "Are you as passionate about the children you care for as felines?"

"Yes."

"Do you express your views with their parents as you have with me?"

Emma wasn't about to lie. She raised her chin. "If warranted."

"What is their response?"

"In one case, I was let go."

"Fired for speaking your mind?"

"I wasn't hired to spout my opinions," she admitted. "But by that point, the only reason I hadn't quit was the children. I was staying on for their sake."

A closed-mouth smile curved his lips. "Lucky kids to have you on their side."

He didn't sound upset. That surprised her. "I do my best, but I expect kids to behave, so maybe they aren't so lucky to have me."

"What happens if they don't behave?"

"Depends on the child. Some kids need to talk it through. Be heard. Others don't understand why they act out." Emma's ability to read people had helped her survive in one foster home after another, but she couldn't read Mr.

Cole. A billionaire shouldn't be interested in her job as a nanny. Maybe one of his colleagues needed to hire child care. "With certain children, more tangible consequences like a time-out or chores are necessary. But I prefer using kindness and a loving hand if at all possible."

"What will my consequence be?"

"Yours?"

"If I misbehave."

Playful images of how he might misbehave flitted through her mind. Unwelcome ones. Ones that made her cheeks burn. "I...I'm your personal assistant. Not your nanny."

"If you were my nanny."

Emma would have to resign due to naughty thoughts. Wrong answer. She cupped the side of her neck with her palm, shaken by her reaction to the sudden change in him. Her skin didn't feel warm to the touch. Maybe only her cheeks were red. But a blush was too much. "Mr. Cole—"

"AJ." His smile, full of sex appeal and devilish charm, stole her breath. "We're going to be working together for the next five days. Putting on a birthday party and surrounded by my family. Humor me, Emma."

Her name rolled off his tongue and heated her insides twenty degrees. A flame reignited deep within her. So not good. And 100 percent unacceptable.

Get a grip. AJ wasn't flirting. A rich, gorgeous man would never be attracted to a simple, unremarkable nanny. More likely he was testing her. Libby had mentioned something about AJ's tests.

A test Emma could handle. She'd been a good student, mostly As, a few Bs. But she'd grown up since then. Emma straightened, book-on-top-of-her-head posture. She had no doubt she would pass this test with an A-plus no matter what Attila threw at her.

She looked across the table at him. Awareness of the man's good looks and power shivered through her. At least she hoped she would pass his test.

Chapter Two

What was Emma thinking? Of course she would pass any test her new boss threw at her. She stared at AJ, seated across from her, noting the devilish smile on his face.

"What would I do if you misbehaved?" She tilted her head to the right and made a stern face, something she rarely used with children. "I'd start by talking to you."

"I'm not a big talker." His mouth quirked, a sexy slant of his lips she tried to ignore. "I prefer action to words."

Libby hadn't called her boss a player, but implied as much. Emma could tell he knew the rules of the game and how to break them. Especially when the game was business. "I imagine you know exactly when you're behaving badly."

"That's part of the fun."

No doubt. "A time-out wouldn't work with you."

"I'd only get into more trouble if I had time to think."

Or he might come up with a way to make another few million dollars. "Then I would do something else."

He leaned forward, a movement full of swagger though he was sitting. "What?"

Emma took her time answering. She studied his hair, lowered her gaze to his intensely focused eyes, followed his straight nose to those sensual lips, then dropped to his strong jaw and square chin. Handsome, yes, but calculating. She made her own assessment of what might mean the most to him. "I'd take away your electronics."

His model-worthy jaw dropped. "What?"

A satisfied smile tugged at the corners of her mouth. Her answer surprised him. Good. "I'd confiscate your cell phone, computer, tablet. That might teach you a lesson."

"Sounds a bit harsh."

"Not if it's for your own good."

He rubbed his chin. "Then I'd better behave."

"Yes, you should." His bank account didn't impress Emma. He didn't, either. Not much anyway. "Don't make me go all Supernanny or Nanny McPhee on you."

The plane lurched.

Here we go. Emma gripped the seat arms and glanced out the window. A small single-propeller aircraft taxied in front of them.

"Please prepare for takeoff," a male voice announced from overhead speakers.

Must be the pilot. Her gaze traveled to AJ. He looked blurry. The rest of the cabin, too. She adjusted her glasses, blinked, but her vision remained fuzzy, the air surrounding her hazy and white.

"Emma?"

She squinted, trying to bring his face and body into focus. "Yes."

"You're pale. Libby told me you don't like flying."

Emma didn't blame her friend for warning her boss.

"It's the moment the wheels lift off that gets to me the most, but I should be okay."

Please let me be okay. The engines revved, louder and louder.

No big deal. She dug her fingers into the butter-soft leather. Pressed her feet against the floor. Leaned her head against the seat.

No big deal. The jet bolted forward, as if released from a slingshot, accelerating down the runway. Dread crept through her stomach and hardened into stone, an uncomfortable heaviness settling in. She burned again, her skin, her insides, immune to the blasts of cool air.

No big deal. Emma squeezed her eyes shut. Darkness didn't keep the sickening, familiar sensation of weightlessness at bay. The moment the wheels lifted, her stomach plummeted to her toes, then boomeranged to her throat.

Memories bombarded her. The choking smell of smoke. The scorching heat of the flames. The terrifying screams of her brother.

Nausea rose inside her like the jet climbing in the sky. She opened her eyes. "Oh, no."

AJ's hands rested on his thighs. "What?"

Emma's stomach constricted. Her mouth watered. She reached into the seat pocket. "I'm going to be sick."

Damn. AJ stared at Emma, who held on to a white barf bag as if it were the Holy Grail. He pushed himself forward in his seat, difficult to do facing backward and strapped in with the plane climbing, but he'd achieved the impossible before.

He reached for her, uncertain how to help, but needing to do something. "Emma."

She raised her left hand, an almost imperceptible movement he took to mean "not now." He didn't blame her, but sitting here unable to do anything brought back a dreaded sense of helplessness, of uselessness. He remembered being out on the water with his father during a storm. More than once AJ figured they would have to abandon ship. More than once he thought they would die. More than once he vowed to do something different with his life if they survived.

You'll never amount to anything if you leave Haley's Bay.

His father's words pounded through AJ's head like high tide against the harbor rocks. He'd spent the past ten years proving his dad wrong. In spades.

Except AJ's private jet, fifteen-hundred employees and a net worth of eleven billion were irrelevant at the moment. None of those things could help Emma.

Her greenish complexion worsened. Her white-knuckled fingers, clutching the barf bag, trembled.

The plane continued climbing. If he unbuckled, he might end up on top of Emma. Better to wait until the plane leveled.

The least he could do was give her privacy. Not easy in this confined space, but he glanced out the window.

Tendrils of fluffy white clouds floated in the blue sky. A good day for flying, unless you suffered airsickness.

A moan filled the cabin.

The cat's stop-they're-torturing-me cry irritated AJ. Who was he kidding? Everything about felines, especially how much bandwidth people wasted posting "cute" cat pictures on the internet, bugged him. He wanted the cat to be a distraction when they reached Haley's Bay, not during the flight. AJ drummed his fingers against the armrest.

Emma's retching stopped. The cat kept howling. He suppressed a groan.

AJ wanted to start his day over. Nothing about his trip

was turning out as expected. He wanted to make a triumphant return to Haley's Bay. He wanted everything to go smoothly during his five-day stay. He wanted Libby with her anal-retentive organizing skills accompanying him, not some…nanny. He'd joked with Emma to see her response and glimpse her social skills.

What in the world was he going to do with an uptight, vomiting Mary Poppins? Libby had warned him about Emma's problem with flying. If he'd known her issue involved bodily fluids, he would have asked his chauffeur Charlie to drive Emma to Haley's Bay instead. A car ride would have been easier on her, on AJ, on the annoying cat.

He flexed his fingers. Libby's brain must have been foggy after her appendectomy. He didn't understand why she thought her best friend was the perfect person to take her place. Emma might be good with kids. She hadn't been bad at bantering. But she didn't seem up for the rigors of the job. Or his family.

Something clicked. The sound came from Emma's direction. He glanced her way.

She held on to the barf bag with one hand and a wipe with the other. Her hands shook. Her face looked deathly white.

AJ's chest tightened. He needed to do something. "I'll call Camille."

"I'm fine." Emma's words sounded strangled. She stared at her lap.

"You need help."

She gave a slight shake of her head, washed her face, then tossed the wipe into the barf bag. "I'm doing better."

Emma removed another wipe from her bag and cleaned her hands. No hesitation, no wasted movement, no hunching her shoulders trying to disappear.

"You're doing great under the circumstances," he said.

Her self-sufficiency and resiliency intrigued AJ. She was no damsel in distress waiting to be rescued by a handsome prince. Not that he was a prince. More like a black knight or the devil himself, according to his father. "But please let Camille assist you. That's her job."

"My job is to assist you, not cause anyone extra work."

AJ studied the woman. Emma Markwell was not unattractive, in spite of her pallor. He would call her... unfinished, an artist's sketch on a piece of canvas waiting to be painted. Her braided hair accentuated her heart-shaped face and clear complexion. Smart-girl glasses hid a pair of wide-set bluish-gray eyes and rested on a straight, pert nose. Tight lines hovered at the corner of her full lips.

Of course they did. She'd thrown up breakfast. But the way she handled herself impressed him. AJ had judged her too quickly and she was earning his respect now. He'd gotten seasick on a boat when he was younger and not handled himself nearly as well. Maybe she was up for the job.

A woman who dressed practically would be a refreshing change from stilettos and tight pencil skirts. The nanny was pretty. If Emma unbraided her brown hair and wore makeup to highlight her cheekbones and lips, she could be beautiful. She lacked the sophistication and worldliness of most women he knew, but a nanny didn't need to dress to impress and show off flawless beauty. He imagined that Emma's fresh young face and prim appearance earned her more jobs than looking like a sexy supermodel. She might not be a high-flying businesswoman, actress or socialite, but she reminded him of the women in his family—down-to-earth, practical, strong. So far she'd been less nosy than his grandmother, mom or sisters. He hoped Emma's lack of interest in his personal life continued.

She tucked another wipe into the airsickness bag, folded the ends, then secured the flap with wired tabs.

Competent and capable. Resilient with an underlying toughness. Those traits would serve her well.

He wondered if she'd been disappointed by someone she loved. Perhaps someone she'd trusted had failed her. AJ's skill at assessing staff had been key to his success, and he understood her qualities from his own experience. Setbacks made you stronger, if you didn't allow them to win. And he knew how to help her. By putting what she needed within reach.

"It's obvious you're fine, but is there anything Camille can bring you? A glass of water? Ginger ale?"

Pink tinged Emma's cheeks, the blush bringing much-needed color to her face. "No, thanks. The plane's no longer climbing. I'm going to go to the lavatory and put myself back together."

She sounded confident, but she hadn't looked him in the eye since being sick. She might not be as in control as she appeared. "The bathroom is at the front of the jet."

Emma's gaze met his. Her vulnerability would have knocked him flat on his ass if he were standing. She was twenty-six, the same age as Libby, but Emma looked younger, like a naive college freshman away from home for the first time.

A protective instinct welled inside him. "Em…"

"Thank you, Mr. Cole."

Her polite tone jerked him back to reality. She didn't want pity. But he wasn't offering that.

She unbuckled her seat belt. He did the same. "Don't feel bad. Libby warned me you didn't like flying. I'm assuming she spoke with Camille about adding airsickness bags to the seats."

"I appreciate Libby's foresight. She's a good friend who

knows me well. I'll do my best to fill her shoes. In spite of the past few minutes, I'm up to the task." Emma stood. She placed the strap of her large purse over her shoulder and held on to the barf bag. "Now if you'll excuse me."

AJ jumped to his feet. She walked past him toward the front of the plane. His gaze followed, zeroing in on the sway of her hips and the purse bouncing against her thigh. Nice. Feminine. Sexy.

Whoa. What was he thinking? He didn't want anything to do with Emma except to comfort and reassure her. He considered employees assets, efficient resources, not playthings. Besides, she reminded him of the girls back in Haley's Bay, rather than the glamorous women he dated in Seattle, San Francisco or wherever else he might be working. The next-door neighbor types weren't the kind of women he was attracted to now. Not that he found Emma...okay, he found her attractive, which surprised him.

With a towel in hand, Camille stood next to his seat. "Emma said she was sick."

"Yes, but remarkably neat about it."

Camille checked the seat and floor anyway. "Libby was right."

"She usually is." He glanced toward the front of the plane. "Make sure Emma is okay."

"Of course."

The cat screeched.

Camille shook her head. "Not your typical uneventful flight."

"No."

Things might not be uneventful until AJ was back home in Seattle. Five days. Five days until his visit would be over. Five days until he would say goodbye to Haley's Bay for another decade. He couldn't wait.

* * *

Emma couldn't wait to get off this airplane. Hitting rock bottom less than fifteen minutes after meeting a new boss had to be a record. But at least things couldn't get worse.

Unless the plane crashed.

She returned her toothbrush to her toiletry bag. Given her luck so far this morning, that was a distinct possibility. But the odds against crashing after throwing up had to be astronomical, right?

Surveying her reflection in the mirror, she tucked stray strands back into her braid. Her Goth-white complexion had disappeared. Good. She would rather look human than like a vampire wannabe.

She pinched her cheeks to give them more color. Reapplying the makeup she'd wiped off was beyond her. But she looked better, passable, no longer green.

She straightened her glasses, wanting to present a confident, unflappable air. Mr. Cole never needed to know she was dying of embarrassment. Neither did Camille, who kept knocking every minute and a half to see if Emma needed help. She opened the lavatory door.

Blossom's ear-hurting screeches could wake the dead, officially starting the zombie apocalypse.

Emma followed the racket.

The cat faced forward, screaming her lungs out as if doing her best T. rex impersonation.

Emma knelt in front of the cat carrier. "Shhhh. I know you don't like this, but we're almost there."

Blossom barked, sounding more like an ankle-biting dog than a pissed-off feline.

"Your cat doesn't sound happy."

Emma felt AJ's presence—a potent mix of heat, strength and confidence—behind her. "Blossom doesn't like to fly, either."

"You look good as new."

She glanced over her shoulder, her gaze at crotch level. Lingering on his zipper. Her cheeks burned. No need for pinching cheeks or makeup now. She looked up at him. "I am. Flying doesn't really get to me. Taking off is the culprit. The weightlessness."

"Your stomach can't handle the feeling."

"Nope." And the flashbacks nearly did her in each time, but nobody needed to know about those. "The landing will be a breeze. But I'm guessing Blossom won't quiet down until she's out of her carrier."

AJ kneeled. The left side of his body brushed hers, sending sparks shooting across her skin. The scent of his aftershave, something musky with a touch of spice, enveloped her.

She sucked in a breath. *Oh, boy.* He smelled so good, fresh, like the first spring day after months of dreary winter rain.

He peered into the carrier. "What's its name again?"

"Blossom. *Her* name is Blossom."

He tapped on the carrier. "Be quiet, Blossom."

"Cat's don't respond to—"

The cat stopped meowing. Blossom rubbed her head against the carrier door.

He stuck his finger through the grating and touched the cat. "Don't respond to what?"

"Logic."

Blossom, however, didn't make another noise. She soaked up the attention. Purred. Unbelievable. The cat hadn't purred at the shelter or at Emma's apartment. At least not that any of the volunteers had noticed. Yet this guy, a non-cat-lover guy, had the feline purring like a generator. "Blossom likes you."

"She likes the attention."

"Attention from you. This is the first time I've heard her purr."

AJ yanked his hand away, plastered his arm against his side. "I'm not a fan of cats. She wouldn't like me."

Tell that to Blossom. The cat pressed against the crate door, fur squishing through the grating. She stared up at AJ as if he were her sun, stars and moon.

Thanks to AJ Cole, Blossom had transformed from she devil to sweetheart. Emma grinned, something she never expected to do after getting sick in front of her new boss. "She does like you."

AJ's gaze bounced from the cat to Emma. "The cat needed someone to tell her what was expected."

"Cats do what they want."

"Perhaps the cat needed to have a higher bar set for its behavior."

He didn't use Blossom's name, but the feline didn't seem to mind. She was trying to get out of the cage and closer to AJ. "Perhaps. But this gives me hope."

"Hope?"

"That Blossom will find her forever home. There's been concern she might be unadoptable. She doesn't seem to like many people."

He looked at Blossom, but he didn't touch her. Much to the cat's dismay. "I don't know anything about cats, but she seems fine to me. Not so annoying now that she's quiet."

Camille approached. She handed AJ a glass with a straw sticking out. "Your protein shake."

"Thanks." His fingers circled the glass.

The flight attendant handed a small juice-sized glass to Emma. "A little ginger ale for you."

"Thank you," Emma said.

"We'll be landing soon." Camille motioned to the back of the plane. "Please return to your seats."

Emma did and buckled her seat belt. The engines whirred. She waited for Blossom to meow, but the cat remained quiet.

AJ sat across from her. Sipped from the straw. "You okay?"

She nodded.

"If you feel bad again, Camille restocked the side pocket."

Two more airsickness bags were inside. "Thanks, but I've never had trouble during landings." At least not the one Emma remembered.

"We're beginning our descent into Haley's Bay," the pilot announced. "Please remain seated."

She gripped the armrests, a combination of anticipation of wanting to be on the ground and apprehension over what the rest of the week would hold.

AJ stared at her over the rim of his glass, his eyes full of concern. "The pilot's very good."

"You don't have to reassure me."

His gaze narrowed, darkened. "Why not?"

"It's not your job."

"I get to write my job description. One benefit of being the boss."

"Do you like being the boss?"

He stiffened. Stared into his drink. Toyed with the straw.

"No one's asked me that. People assume…" He shifted in his seat. "But yes, of course. What's not to love?"

He was bluffing, hiding something, like a child who said swim lessons were fun when dunking his head under water terrified him. What other secrets was AJ hiding?

None of Emma's business. She didn't need to go looking for AJ Cole's demons. She had enough of her own. But she hoped this vacation went well for him because the only thing worse than having no family would be having a family that didn't get along. Best to make sure she knew what AJ needed from her.

She removed a half-inch binder and a mechanical pencil from her tote bag. "Libby sent me your tentative itinerary. Any changes to today's schedule I should know about?"

He waved his hand, as if brushing aside Emma's question. "Relax until we land."

"Let's confirm today's agenda first." She adjusted her glasses. "Then I'll relax."

AJ took another sip of his drink. "Read what's on your list."

"Lunch with your grandmother while I arrange meetings with the party rental company and florist and check into the Broughton Inn. A conference call at two, another one at three, followed by an interview at four with a technology blogger. Then you have a break until dinner with your family at seven."

"Easy afternoon."

"Three calls on the first afternoon of your vacation sounds more like you're working."

He raised a brow, as if surprised by her words. Guess Libby didn't speak to him like that. Well, Emma wasn't like her best friend. Not even close.

"This is a light day." He placed his empty glass on the table between them. "I've limited what's on my schedule."

Emma guessed she had a different definition of limited from his. "If there aren't any changes—"

"There is one."

She readied her pencil.

A muscle ticked at his jaw.

She leaned forward. "What?"

"We're staying at my grandmother's house. It'll be easier with the party planning, and my grandma thought it would be better for the cat."

Disappointment shot through Emma. She'd been a live-in nanny so she knew what staying at someone's house as an employee meant. But the arrangement made sense, even without the cat factored in. She pasted on a smile. "That's generous of your grandmother."

He leaned back against his seat, but his gaze never left her. "My grandmother loves playing hostess. She's thrilled I'm bringing company, not to mention a cat."

The noise level of the engines changed. She clasped her hands together. "I'm sure your grandmother's more excited to have you staying with her. Ten years is a long time to be away."

"What has Libby told you?"

"Not much." A glance out the window told Emma the plane was descending. "I know you're throwing your grandmother an eightieth birthday party. Very nice of you to do."

"Just holding up my end of a deal."

Emma looked back at him. "Excuse me?"

His gaze, warm and clear, met hers. "When I was eight, I wanted a space-alien birthday party. My dad said no, so my grandma offered to throw me a party if I agreed to do the same for her when she turned eighty. We shook on it."

Emma tried to picture AJ as a boy, but looking past the handsome man sitting across from her was impossible. "You remembered that after all these years?"

"No." He half laughed. The charming sound sent a brush of tingles across Emma's tummy. "My grandma did. She reminded me in February."

She rubbed her stomach. Maybe she was feeling the after-effects of being sick earlier. "Still nice of you."

"She's my grandma. I wasn't about to say no."

"Would you be returning to Haley's Bay if it weren't her birthday?"

"Probably not, which she knows." Affection filled his gaze. "My grandmother's a sly one. But I'm on my way so she's happy. I want the party to go smoothly. That's what I'm counting on you for, Emma."

She wrote the words "anticipate and prevent problems" in her binder. "Yes, Mr. Cole."

"AJ."

The man had seen her vomit. The only other people to see her do that were her parents, God rest their souls, and Libby. "AJ."

He smiled. She smiled back. The moment lingered. Filled her with heat. She looked at her binder. "Anything else I should know?"

"My family is big and crazy and loud." AJ sounded amused, not annoyed. "I have four brothers—Ellis, Flynn, Declan and Grady—and two sisters—Bailey and Camden. Not to mention my sister-in-law, Risa, and more aunts, uncles and cousins than I can count."

"That is a big family."

"The single Cole men will hit on you because you're new in town and their reputations haven't been sullied yet. They've done that in the past. You're under no obligation to them, and let me know if they annoy you." AJ's dark eyes and serious tone told Emma he wasn't joking. "What you do on your own time is none of my business, but don't let your actions affect your ability to get the job done."

His words irritated her. Okay, he didn't know her, but she wasn't about to sleep around because good-looking guys were giving her attention. She imagined his brothers were attractive, AJ in multiples, like the Hemsworth brothers. That could be dangerous. To her job and her heart. She jotted a note in the margin. "Stay away from Cole males."

"I'll keep my distance."

A lopsided grin formed. "Smart."

She hated the way her body responded to his compliment. "It's been my experience that business and pleasure don't mix well."

"Mine, too."

At least they agreed on something.

"But business has to be fun," AJ added. "All work and no play…"

"Would be boring." Emma recalled Libby's description of the Cole corporate headquarters in Seattle with a game arcade, gym, massages, errand service, and free meals, snacks and drinks at the employee cafeterias. *Fun* seemed to be the operative word at his company. Not surprising given that he developed a photography-based blogging platform and created a social media gaming site for friends to compete. "I wouldn't last long as a nanny if I didn't play. Having fun means everything to children."

"What about you?"

"I like to have fun."

He drummed his fingers against the chair arm. "What do you do for fun?"

"Play tag, dress-up, bicycle, hunt for treasure, bake, board games, and go to the Oregon Zoo, the children's museum or OMSI."

His fingers stilled. "I meant what do *you* do when you're not being a nanny."

"Oh. Sorry. I like to read, watch movies, hike, volunteer at an animal rescue center."

"Quiet pleasures."

"It's not always quiet at the rescue shelter, but the noise is different there. I love being a nanny. The children are wonderful, but they're loud and full of energy and want your undivided attention. A little quiet is nice."

"Alone time is fun for you."

She bit back a smile. AJ wasn't grilling her, but he seemed to want to know more about her. She would have expected a billionaire to brag and make sure the conversation centered around him. Not that she knew any billionaires, but she'd worked for a millionaire. "Escaping inside a dark theater with a bucket of popcorn, a soda, a box of candy and no one to take to the bathroom at the best part of a movie is the definition of superfun."

"There's a theater in Haley's Bay."

"Thanks, but I doubt you'll be screaming and tugging on my shirt to get attention all day long."

"No screaming." He winked. "And I've found persuading a woman to take off her shirt works better than tugging."

"I'm surprised you have to persuade them." The man's smile could charm a snake out of its skin. "I assumed women flashed you, like at Mardi Gras."

"Only in my dreams." With a wry grin, he settled back in his seat. "But they're very nice dreams."

"I imagine so."

"What do you dream about, Emma?"

"I... Um, a lot of things."

"Like what?"

She fiddled with her seat belt. "Cats. Children. Family."

"Nanny things?"

A lump the size of a Super Ball burned in Emma's throat. She swallowed, kept her smile from wavering and looked AJ straight in the eyes. "Yes, nanny things."

Cat lover things. Mommy things. Wife things. Things a man who had a family, albeit an estranged one, would never understand. Things she dreamed about. Things she wanted...desperately.

Chapter Three

Charlie, AJ's chauffeur for three years, cut five minutes off the drive from the minuscule airport to Haley's Bay. AJ rubbed his thumb against his fingertips.

He liked being on time. He preferred arriving early. Charlie was doing his job, getting AJ to his destination as quickly as possible. But this once, he wouldn't have minded being late.

Still, he didn't lower the glass panel and tell Charlie to slow down. Not until AJ had a reason, one beyond his wanting to prolong the inevitable.

Music played from the speakers. Stock quotes ran across the bottom of a television screen. The bar called to him, but he needed to be stone-cold sober when he faced his family. AJ glanced at Emma, seated next to him, the cat carrier at her feet.

She stared out the window. Her serious expression— dare he say dour—took prim and proper to the next level.

So different from how she'd been right before landing. Her sense of humor had disappeared. Her smile, too.

She might be upset over getting sick earlier. She might be nervous about her new job. Or she might be acting the way she always did. Whatever the reason, she was his employee, his responsibility. The least he could do was help her relax after a rough flight and coax a smile out of her. "Let's take a detour. Check out a lighthouse or two."

Her lips twisted. "You're expected at your grandmother's house."

"I wouldn't be a gracious host if I didn't show you the sights."

"You're not my host," she countered. "You're my boss."

Being her employer was easy to forget. Libby had hired Emma. "I don't mind playing tour guide."

Her nose crinkled. "You have a schedule—"

"Subject to change."

"True, but as your personal assistant I'm supposed to keep you on schedule."

"True, but you're also supposed to do what I ask."

"Even if doing so isn't in your best interest? I mean, you haven't been home in ten years. Your grandmother might be peeking out the window waiting for you to arrive."

He pictured Grandma doing that. "I'll concede the point."

"Thank you."

"You're welcome."

His gaze met Emma's. She removed her glasses to blow on the right lens. Pretty blue eyes surrounded by long, thick lashes. He hadn't noticed her eyelashes before. "Does your grandmother do the same when you visit?"

"My grandparents are dead." Emma put on her glasses and stared out the window. "Looks like we're here."

A wooden sign on the side of the two-lane road welcomed visitors to Haley's Bay. The sign was new. The churning in AJ's stomach wasn't.

After a decade, the town had likely changed. In that same time, his life had also changed. His family's opinion of him might never change. That could take a century. Or longer.

The last time he was home his family had tried to shame him into staying in Haley's Bay. That wouldn't happen again, but something else might. He wanted to be prepared. "One of your responsibilities is running interference for me."

"What do you mean?"

"If I find myself in a difficult situation, I may need you to get me out of it by texting or calling or physically interrupting me."

She smiled at the sleeping cat before looking up at him. "Afraid you might run into old girlfriends who might want to rekindle the flame?"

"That isn't likely to happen." His high school sweetheart and ex-fiancée, Natalie, had dumped him and married one of his closest friends. AJ had been devastated, but recovered. A good lesson learned—immediate gratification was more important than loyalty to some people. "But there will be people around. My family, too."

Emma eyed him warily. "Family?"

He nodded once. "Libby and I have a code word. If I text or say the word, she knows to take action."

Emma removed her notepad from her bag. "What's the code word?"

"Top secret."

"If I don't know what to listen for, I'm not going to be able to help you."

He rubbed his chin. "We need our own word. Something obscure, but not too random."

Emma tapped her pen against her notepad. "How about…lighthouse?"

AJ mulled over the suggestion. Ten letters would be a bear to text, but the word could be worked into a conversation without sounding like a non sequitur.

"That'll work." Satisfaction flowed through him. The word played perfectly into his plans. "To make sure we remember the code word, we'll visit one now."

"No need. I'll remember."

"A few hours spent sightseeing won't make a difference."

"What's really going on?" She studied him. "You remind me of a kid trying to put off going to the doctor's for a shot."

His jaw tensed. "I'm not scared of needles."

"You're scared of something."

Emma's insight made him squirm. She had zero qualms pinpointing and commenting on what was going on in his head, trying to fix what was upsetting him. He was used to having people try to fix things for him, but not with nurturing concern, as if she really cared. AJ didn't like it.

"I'm not scared of anything." The words flowed quickly, one after the other without any breaks. Not like him. But then again, he was back in Haley's Bay. That changed everything. "Okay, that's not quite true. The threat of an EMP, electronic magnetic pulse, making every electrical device obsolete has given me nightmares."

"You're not scared about coming home?"

"Nope." Damn. He sounded like a kid, a scared little kid trying to put on a good front, and Emma seemed to know that. "I lived here for eighteen years. I might be a little on edge, but that's because I haven't been here in a while."

"Ten years is a long time."

"I've been busy." A stupid excuse, but she didn't need

to know the real reasons. "But I'm free now. Let's take in a few sights on our way. This is my first vacation in over a year."

Emma's not-going-to-happen-on-my-watch shake of her head stopped him cold. "You'll have a free block of time after your calls this afternoon," she said. "Plenty of time to see the sights over the next five days."

Her friendly tone, as though she was using extra patience for her recalcitrant charge, made him feel like an idiot for bringing this up again. He must be back in his hometown. He'd felt like the village idiot living here.

Emma leaned toward the limousine window. The shift of position brought a whiff of her citrus shampoo—grapefruit or maybe lemon. The fresh scent appealed to him like the nanny.

"Wow." She pressed closer to the glass. "This place is beautiful."

He followed her gaze to the sparkling expanse of water and the heart of the town hugging the shoreline. Pride welled. Foolish, irrepressible pride he buried in a no-nonsense response. "The town hugs the waterfront. Most of the shops and restaurants are on Bay Street near the harbor."

"Is Haley's Bay named after an original settler?"

"Yes." AJ didn't know if she was making conversation or wanted to know the answer. Given her occupation, he'd guess the latter. She seemed the type to pay attention and ask questions of white-haired docents leading museum tours. He wouldn't mind taking her through a couple of the historic sites around here. "Haley was a trader who anchored in the bay during his voyages. That's according to the Lewis and Clark expedition. The bay was renamed Baker Bay, after a British merchant, but the original town name stuck."

"You know your history."

Her praise made him sit taller. A stupid reaction, but returning to his hometown was a stupid move. He should have thrown a royal extravaganza for his grandmother on his turf, in Seattle. Rented the Space Needle. Staged a massive fireworks display. But she'd wanted the party here in the town where she'd been born and lived her entire life. "I learned Washington state history in school, but the old folks around here bring the past alive, especially the fishermen. They love sharing every legend about Haley's Bay."

"I'm usually the one telling stories. I'd love to hear some tales."

The excitement in her voice made him want to offer to introduce her around. Talk about a stupid move. She would be more welcome here than him. But something about Emma made AJ want to help her. Maybe he was feeling sorry for her after the rough flight, but he didn't like it. She worked for him, not the other way around.

"Make friends with the locals," he suggested. "You'll hear them all."

"Must have been fun growing up here."

"When I was a little kid." He studied the buildings—stores and cafés he didn't recognize—along the inland side of Bay Road. Maybe that would take his mind off the woman sitting next to him. A wrought iron wind vane of a sailboat faced west. On the sidewalk, two people walked hand in hand. An unleashed golden retriever trotted next to them. "Not so much when I became a teenager."

"It's a charming town."

"If you like small and boring."

"I do." She stared across him. Her lips parted, spreading into a wide grin that made him want to smile. "Look at the boats."

Sailboat masts teetered on the harbor. Flags fluttered in

the breeze. Empty moorings meant most boats had headed out to sea for the day. "Fishing used to support this town. Now I hear the biggest catch is tourists. A couple of my brothers take them deep sea fishing."

That must kill his dad, who believed the only way to make money was building boats and catching fish. He'd called tourists "barnacles" and a few other choice words he wouldn't say in front of his wife or mother.

With her eager gaze, Emma looked like a tourist herself. All she needed was a camera, sunglasses and a guidebook. "I could see coming here for vacation."

He'd taken days off work, but he couldn't relax here. Still, talking about Haley's Bay with Emma wasn't so bad. Being so aware of her movements and expressions, however, was making him uncomfortable. He focused on the town's geography. "Cape Disappointment is next door with campsites, yurts and hiking trails. There's the Lewis and Clark Interpretive Center. Long Beach is a coastal resort community to the northwest and Astoria, Oregon, is south across the Columbia River. I guess if I hadn't grown up here…"

"You'd come for fun."

"I might." AJ tried hard not to think of this place. "But I always thought of Haley's Bay as the place I couldn't wait to leave when I went to college."

"Back east, right?"

Libby must have prepped Emma with his background info. He assumed only the basics. All he knew about Emma was that she'd been in the foster care system before moving in with Libby and her parents during high school. "MIT."

"Boston must have been a big change with the crowds and skyscrapers."

"My first week it took me three days to fall asleep because of the noise, but I loved living there. Compared to a city, this place is dead."

"You might view your hometown differently now that you're an adult." Emma pointed to the Captain's Café, a multistory restaurant complete with weathered front, crow's nest, anchor and captain's wheel. "Do they have good food?"

"I've never seen the place." He searched his memory for what had been there before. The doughnut shop, no... that wasn't right. "That used to be Stu's Sandwich Shop, a hole-in-the-wall storefront. But no one could top their pastrami on rye."

"I love a good Reuben."

AJ imagined her biting into a big sandwich, a dab of Thousand Island on the corner of her mouth. He wouldn't mind licking it off and tasting more than the dressing.

Whoa. Where had that come from? He didn't lick, let alone kiss, employees.

And she was his employee. Smart. Observant with journalist-writing-a-travel-piece insights, opinions and questions. Qualities he searched for when hiring staff. The other things he looked for were initiative and loyalty. Always, after what he'd gone through in Haley's Bay, loyalty.

She gestured to the passing scenery, giving him another whiff of her shampoo. "What other places are new?"

Ignoring how good she smelled, he took in the street, noting the differences from his memory to reality. "The Coffee Shack, Donut Heaven, Bert's Hardware, the Bay Mercantile Store and the barbershop were here before, but the building facades are updated. The Candy Cave, the Buried Treasure and Raging Waters are new. They appear more for tourists than locals. But I'll bet the new store owners have the same small-town mentality as everyone else."

"That so-called mentality is part of the appeal."

Her odd—almost disapproving?—expression jabbed at him. Libby wasn't a yes-person, but if her opinion differed from his she wasn't vocal like Emma. The nanny had no problem speaking up. He wasn't used to people doing so and wasn't sure if he liked it or not. "The mentality is difficult to take growing up."

"You feel that way, but many people didn't grow up in a small town. They want to experience what that's like. That's why tourists like visiting. Haley's Bay has to be a popular destination or we'd see the effects of a down-turned economy, empty businesses and for lease signs in the windows."

Interesting. A nanny with a keen sense of business. She wasn't a carbon copy of Libby, and that was surprisingly okay. He leaned toward Emma, wanting to know more about her. "What was your major in college?"

"I didn't go to college." Not an ounce of regret sounded in her voice. She raised her chin with a hint of pride and determination, two more traits that appealed to him. "I attended a thirty-month nanny certification program in Portland. But I loved my economics class in high school. I like to read and stay up on current events. Nannies are a child's second teacher, after their parents. I aim to enhance a child's natural interests."

Initiative in the flesh, plus confidence and curiosity. All packaged as a prim, proper, mousy nanny who had a pretty smile when she let it show. Emma would work out nicely. The more she dealt with, the more he could retreat.

"You might not like your hometown, but I love the quaint shops and cafés." She rested her head against the back of the seat, her shoulder brushing his. "Quintessential Pacific Northwest coastal town."

Her wistful, romantic tone annoyed him. So did the tin-

gle racing down his arm from where she'd touched him.
"Forest and water, Emma. Please. Don't get all rose-tinted
on me, okay? This is Hicksville and being here held me
back, badly. I never would have amounted to anything if
I'd stayed in Haley's Bay. This place was suffocating."

The words rushed from his mouth before he could stop
them. He'd never said these thoughts before. Weird. He
was more careful and reserved around strangers. Around
people he knew, too.

She tilted her head, attention fixed on him. Her focus
unsettled him. He was used to being deferred to. Most
bosses were. Emma must not have gotten the memo.

Of course she hadn't. She consulted with parents and
left when they didn't agree. A free agent unused to following the chain of command. Like him when he'd started
his business. How unexpected.

"What?" he asked finally.

"You…" She pursed her lips, full and unglossed.

He prepared for a lecture. Wanted to hear what she had
to say if she didn't drag on for more than a minute or so.

"…couldn't have done a better job at getting away and
making something of yourself."

The praise filled him with unexpected warmth. Most
people complimented him, but AJ never knew if they
meant the words or were trying to suck up to him. Emma
didn't seem to be the kind of person to belong in that second group. "Thanks. There's more—"

She nodded to him, as if encouraging him to continue.
"More what?"

Damn. AJ balled one of his hands. He didn't know why
he kept telling Emma things. He didn't let his guard down
around anyone, friend or employee. Fresh-smelling hair
and pretty smile aside.

"More I want to do. Places to visit." Not what he intended to say, but the words were true and the perfect way to change the subject. "Are there places you'd like to travel?"

"Anywhere."

"In the world?"

She nodded. "The farthest from Portland I've been is Puerto Vallarta. It's hard to get around the flying."

"You flew today."

"To help Libby." Emma's gaze returned to the view out the window. The limousine followed the road along the bay toward his grandmother's house. "I should have suggested driving myself and meeting you here, but I was so worried about Libby I wasn't thinking straight."

He knew the feeling being with Emma. "When it's time for you to return to Portland, my driver will take you home."

She glanced around the limousine, taking in the multiple screens, leather seats, bar. "This is your, um, car."

AJ nodded. "Charlie drove down from Seattle this morning. I never intended on flying to Haley's Bay, but I didn't want to leave Libby alone in New York. She's too valuable to me. If I'd known she hadn't been feeling well before we'd left on the trip, I never would have taken her along, but she hid her abdominal pains until they became acute. I waited for her mother to arrive, made sure she was settled and comfortable, then flew here with a couple stops along the way."

"Oh."

The surprise in the one word spoke volumes. Emma Markwell had thought the worst of him. She wasn't the only one, especially here in Haley's Bay. "You assumed I left Libby in the hospital alone."

"Maybe."

"That means yes."

Emma stared up at him through her eyeglasses, her cheeks red and a contrite look on her face. "It's nice to know you didn't. Leave Libby, that is."

Not a full compliment, but better than being slammed for something he didn't do. Still, he liked the idea of making Emma squirm since she'd done the same to him. "You're backpedaling."

"Not really."

"I'm a nice guy."

Emma raised an arched brow. "Are you always nice?"

Damn. "I try to be."

"Trying doesn't always work."

"No, but I can tell myself I didn't set out to be a jerk."

"Is this something you tell yourself often?" she teased.

Her sense of humor had returned. She would need every funny bone with his family. "You'll be able to answer that question on Sunday."

"That sounds like I should be worried."

"Maybe."

Emma laughed. "Guess I deserve that."

The limousine pulled to a stop. The engine turned off.

AJ glanced to his right. His grandmother's Victorian stood peacock-blue and proud across a lawn of manicured grass and blooming flower beds. His heart beat like a halyard on a mast. "We're here."

"Wow. Your grandmother's home is perfect. Even with the water right here, the house is what shines."

He recognized the awe in Emma's voice. A familiar sense of reverence—of home—brought an unexpected smile to his face. "The house has been in our family for generations."

Emma's eyes widened. "That's a long time to stay in one place."

"Coles have lived in Haley's Bay since the Civil War."

Her gaze bounced from the house to him. "The house isn't that old."

"My great grandfather bought the house ninety years ago. He liked the view of the bay."

"Let me guess, he was a fisherman."

"And boat builder."

Emma looked over her shoulder at the bay. She took her time, allowed her gaze to absorb what she saw. "Lovely."

The dreamy haze in her eyes and a soft smile on her face made her lovely, too. He shook the thought from his head. "The view from the second floor is better. You can see the harbor."

Charlie opened the door.

AJ motioned for Emma to go first.

She slung her bag over her shoulder and clasped the plastic handle on the cat carrier. Moving toward the open door, she looked like she might topple out of the car. He didn't need her to get hurt. One personal assistant in the hospital was enough.

He took the carrier from her. "I've got the cat."

Her gaze met his then she looked away. "Thank you."

AJ followed her out and stood on the sidewalk. Vividly painted terra-cotta flowerpots full of colorful pink, purple and yellow blossoms sat on each step leading to the wraparound porch. His sister Bailey's creations, he was sure, the sight comforting as his grandma's crocheted afghans. He only hoped his dad wasn't part of the welcoming committee.

AJ gestured to the steps. "After you."

Halfway up, Emma stopped. "There's a swing."

The breathless quality to her voice surprised him. He peered around her to see the white slotted-back, two-person bench hanging from thick silver chains. "Looks like my grandmother replaced her old swing. She used to love to drink tea out here and watch the boats. Guess she still does."

"We had a swing." Emma took the last two stairs. "Boy, did we abuse that thing. My mom got so mad at us."

A bright, toothpaste-ad smile lit up her face.

AJ's chest tightened. Emma looked so lighthearted and happy. She should smile more.

He joined her on the porch. "Us?"

Something—not panic, perhaps surprise—flashed in her eyes. "My, um, older brother."

"My younger brothers and I played on Grandma's old swing all the time. Had to fix it more than once after climbing and hanging off the chains." He set the cat carrier on the porch. "We used to stand on the backrest and swing to see how high we could go. We also jumped off the seat to see if we could clear the porch rail and bushes."

She leaned over the rail as if estimating the distance down to the lawn. "Sounds dangerous."

He bit back a laugh. "You sound like a nanny."

"Occupational hazard." Her amused gaze met his. "But you can't tell me no one got hurt."

He pointed under his chin. "I have a scar to show for the fun we had. My youngest brother, Grady, has two."

"Your poor grandmother."

"She didn't mind. Now our mom—"

The front door opened.

"You're here." His grandma stood in the doorway. She wore a pair of light blue pants and a white peasant blouse. All five feet of short gray curls and sharp blue eyes barreled toward him like a stampeding water buffalo, albeit a baby one. "You're finally home."

Not his home. He lived in Seattle. But the excitement in her voice reminded AJ that this visit wasn't about him.

AJ hugged his grandmother. Her rose-scented perfume

smelled sweeter than when she'd visited him in Seattle. "It's not like you gave me a choice, Grandma."

She tsked, stepped back and assessed him from head to toe. "I like the long hair, but you need the ends trimmed. Go visit Monty at the barbershop. He'll fix you right up."

AJ shook his head. "Nice to see you, too, Grandma."

Emma laughed under her breath.

"Grandmother." He motioned to his new assistant, who stood with a patient smile on her face and her arm half-extended toward his grandmother. "I'd like you to meet—"

"Is he here?" A high-pitched female voice called from inside the house. "Grandmother Cole? Is he?"

"AJ is here." Grandma leaned closer, lowering her voice. "Risa has been waiting for you to arrive all morning. Her youngest sister is here, too. And she can't wait to meet the illustrious and incredibly wealthy AJ Cole."

Danger-up-ahead infused his grandmother's tone. His gut clenched. He'd heard about his sister-in-law's match-making from his sister Bailey. Two brothers and his youngest sister, Camden, had been targeted over the holidays last year, making Thanksgiving and Christmas dinners uncomfortable. "I thought her sister lived far away."

"Hawaii," Grandma said. "But I suppose meeting a billionaire was worth the expense of a trip to the mainland."

Crap. AJ blew out a puff of air. Matchmaking friends and relatives were as bad as a case of chicken pox. Enough women wanted a piece of his bank account. He didn't need an in-law giving one of her sisters a push or inside access to him. On a rare vacation. That he already dreaded. This was not-not-not going to happen.

Grandma shook Emma's hand. "You're Libby?"

"Emma," she said. "Emma Markwell."

Grandma's white eyebrows drew together. Her surprised gaze shot from Emma to him. "I thought your assistant was coming with you."

"Emma is my—"

"AJ." Risa exited the house, her blond ponytail bouncing in the back and a wide smile on her face. She wore a pair of black yoga pants, two pink fitted T-shirts and tennis shoes. "Welcome back to Haley's Bay."

AJ hugged her. She was thin and pretty, a first grade teacher turned stay-at-home mom. They'd met in Seattle a few times, but never with his brother Ellis present. "Nice to see you. How are the kids?"

"Growing so fast I feel old. They'll be by tonight to see their long-lost uncle. But right now there's someone I want you to meet." Risa pointed to the front door where a twentysomething woman with long blond hair struck a sexy pose. "This is my little sister Madison. She lives in Hawaii."

"Hello, AJ." The woman's husky voice sounded like she needed an inhaler. He wouldn't be surprised given the skintight, oh-so-short cocktail dress she wore. Her outfit, complete with stiletto heels showing off toned long legs, was more appropriate for a hip dance club than lunch at his grandmother's house. The two sisters resembled each other, but Madison's looks were harder edged, hyper-athletic compared to stay-at-home, happily married Risa. "Nice to meet you. I've heard so much about you."

AJ knew nothing about Madison. He hadn't been at Risa and Ellis's wedding, though AJ had paid for the reception, his gift to his brother. But one glance told AJ what this sex kitten was offering. Beauty up front, claws in his back. "All good, I hope."

She batted her eyelashes and leaned into the doorway, giving him a flash of her black lace bra. "Of course."

"I can't believe the two of you are in Haley's Bay at the

same time. I thought you could show Madison around. The town has changed a bit since you've been here last, but you can have fun exploring together." Risa's gaze flew between her sister and him so fast he thought she might end up with whiplash. "You have lots in common."

Madison nodded, reminding him of a bobblehead doll. "I love computers."

Right. He'd bet anything she loved the attention she got through Facebook and Instagram by posting selfies snapped in the mirror, posing as though she was a supermodel. AJ pressed his lips together.

"You'll have a good time with Madison," Risa encouraged.

AJ had no doubt about that. But he also knew Madison's type. She might claim to want only a casual fling or relationship, but the I-will-stop-at-nothing-to-win-the-lotto-jackpot-standing-in-front-of-me look in the woman's green eyes gave her away.

AJ inched closer to Emma, who remained quiet with a pleasant smile on her face. He wanted to stay far, far away from Madison. Oh, he'd dated women like her. Casually for a good time. She was his type—a go-getter. But when those women tried to sink their fingernails into him, he disentangled himself. That made Madison more than just an inconvenience because she was his sister-in-law's sister. He had enough family trouble without adding more. If he wasn't careful, Risa's misguided matchmaking could ruin not only his vacation in Haley's Bay, but also his grandmother's birthday. "Sounds fun, but I'm going to be busy planning Grandma's birthday."

"Not that busy," Risa countered, much to Madison's delight. His sister-in-law motioned to Emma. "You brought your assistant to do most of the work. Libby, isn't it?"

Emma's smile didn't waver. "I'm Emma."

The two sisters exchanged a confused glance. Madison frowned.

If only he could keep the woman frowning. Okay, not really. This wasn't personal. Ordinarily he'd be up for hanging with Madison. But he couldn't under the circumstances.

AJ's gaze jumped from Emma to Madison. Two women couldn't be more different. Emma might not be drop-dead sexy in a hot dress, but she was pretty with her girl-next-door looks and practical outfit. Emma wasn't on the hunt for a rich husband so she could live a life of luxury. She worked hard caring for other people's children, taking in homeless cats and helping out her best friend. Some men might want a Madison on their arms. He had, but Emma was the type of woman to bring home to meet the family.

The thought gave AJ an idea, a bad, stupid idea. Nah, he couldn't do that.

With a pointed stare at Emma, Risa's arched brows lifted. "And you're…"

Emma kept smiling. "I'm AJ's—"

"Girlfriend," AJ interrupted, realizing stupid or not, he had no other choice. "Emma is my girlfriend."

One beat. Two. He waited for God to strike him down for lying. Nothing. The Big Man must understand. Desperate times, desperate measures. He stole a glance at Emma.

She looked pained but held her smile in place. Atta girl. Team AJ all the way.

His gaze pleaded, begged her to play along. "Emma is a fan of lighthouses. This trip is the perfect opportunity for her to check them out and meet the family."

He hoped she remembered the code word. If not…

"AJ's girlfriend!" His grandmother hugged Emma. "I'm sorry I assumed you were his assistant. How long have you been dating?"

He bit the inside of his mouth. "I…"

"Not long," Emma finished for him. The way a helpful personal assistant would. Or a girlfriend. "But it feels like—"

"Forever," AJ said.

Even Madison sighed.

The lines on Grandma's forehead deepened. "Why didn't you introduce us when I visited last month?"

"I live in Portland," Emma said, thankfully keeping the charade going.

He nodded. "A long-distance relationship."

"Well, this is simply wonderful." Grandma clapped, then pointed to the cat carrier. "I must admit I didn't know what to think when AJ said there'd be a cat coming, but I figured it was none of my business. What's your cat's name, Emma?"

Emma's smile was more saccharine than sugar. "Blossom. She's a foster cat, but if everything works out as we hope, she'll soon belong to AJ."

What? The scheming, quick-thinking minx. Blackmail. Unbelievable.

He would adopt that pathetic feline over his dead body. But if Emma didn't play along with this charade, he might find himself in an early grave. He was a firm believer in quid pro quo. He pasted on an aspartame smile. "That's right."

Grandma's gaze narrowed. She eyed him suspiciously. "But you don't like cats."

Damn. He took a quick breath, hoping for the right words to say. "I didn't. But that's before I started dating a crazy cat lady."

Emma stiffened then moved closer. Wrapped her hand around his arm. Pinched him.

Ouch.

She waved her fingers. "That would be me. Crazy about cats and lighthouses."

Risa and Madison sized up and glared at Emma. If looks could kill, the two sisters would be behind bars and he'd be hitting up a temp agency to find a new assistant. Time to put an end to Madison's flirting.

AJ removed himself from Emma's hand, then placed his arm around her. Her muscles tensed beneath his palm. But he was more interested in her thin waist and the curve of her hips hidden by her clothes. His pulse kicked up. His temperature spiked. "And I'm crazy about you."

More likely just crazy. All he could think about doing was pulling her closer and kissing her hard on the lips.

Don't make me go all Supernanny or Nanny McPhee on you.

AJ had a feeling kissing Emma might be worth whatever trouble he got into and any punishment she might dish out. Even taking away his electronics.

Chapter Four

Forget the code word. AJ had lost his mind. Eccentric or certifiably insane? That was the question Emma needed to answer before this crazy idea of his went any further. Well, once they were alone. Until then she would act like a dutiful employee. Make that, um, girlfriend.

She followed Mrs. Cole—AJ's grandmother—up the stately Victorian's wide staircase trying not to burst out laughing. Emma Markwell the girlfriend of a hot internet billionaire? Yeah, right. No way could they pull this off. Okay, maybe he could, but not her.

Agreeing to be in a fake relationship with her temporary boss was not going to end well. The logistics of staying in the same house with him were bad enough, but Libby's reaction when she found out about the charade... That would not be pretty.

Emma expected yelling, followed by the silent treatment. Her insides twisted. She loved Libby like a sister.

Upsetting her best friend was not an option. Keeping quiet about the situation was key.

No one outside of Haley's Bay and the Cole family could know about the so-called dating. Now or after the fact. If, and it was a big if, Emma didn't put a stop to the entire thing before someone else called them on the relationship farce. No one, including Libby, would ever believe AJ Cole would date a boring, quiet nanny, let alone take her home to meet his estranged family.

Emma's stomach hurt with an icky, sinking feeling. Not even the scent of lemons and wood polish eased her discomfort. The pewter-framed family photographs covering the walls pressed home all the ways she didn't belong here.

She recognized AJ in several of the pictures. A younger AJ, bearded and happy. He was going to be upset when this lie exploded in his face. Of course it was his fault, but she sympathized with the guy over his sister-in-law's not-so-subtle matchmaking. The fix-up vibe had been strong out on the porch. AJ must be deluged with desiring women.

That would make her unusual in his world. The antithesis to a woman like Madison. Though the pretty woman earned points for being able to walk in such high heels. No way Emma could wear those without ending up face-first on the ground.

Mrs. Cole's thin, veined hand ran along the carved mahogany banister. She glanced over her shoulder at Emma. "How did you meet my grandson?"

"Through Libby." The muscles around Emma's mouth hurt from forcing a smile, but she assumed a girlfriend would look happy while on vacation with her *boyfriend*. Her stomach churned. She was a horrible liar, something AJ would have known if he had mentioned his idea to her first rather than telling her at the same time as everyone one else. She touched her tummy, trying to calm the nausea. "She's been my best friend since freshman year of high school."

That much was true. Emma didn't want to think about pertinent details such as the fact that she and AJ had met only a couple hours ago and he was paying her for her services and...

"Bet Libby gets a big bonus from my grandson for introducing you," Mrs. Cole said.

"Let's hope so." Unless Emma screwed this up. Highly likely. She'd dated, but never seriously and never a rich and powerful man such as AJ Cole. Playing make-believe with children was one thing. She could be a princess, queen, fairy godmother, pirate and ninja with the best of them. Being a pretend girlfriend would take acting abilities she didn't possess. Since this had been AJ's idea, maybe he wouldn't hold her failures against Libby. Emma crossed her fingers. "Libby works hard every day. She deserves a bonus and a raise."

"My employees are well-compensated," AJ said behind Emma. "A happy, satisfied staff makes for a more productive work environment."

If that was his goal, he was failing. Big-time. Emma was not happy or satisfied. She was peeved at being put into the position of lying to his family and friends. She glanced over her shoulder.

AJ's lips pressed together in a thin line. His dark brows furrowed, yet gratitude shone in his eyes. He mouthed the words *thank you,* surprising her.

"I was going to put you in bedrooms down the hall from each other, but that was before I knew you were dating." Mrs. Cole stood on the landing. "There's no reason you can't share a room."

"You don't have to do that." The words rushed from Emma's mouth, matching the panic coursing through her.

Her gaze bounced between AJ and his grandmother. "I mean… This is your house. Separate bedrooms are fine."

Preferred. Emma rubbed her hands together, her blood pressure spiraling with each passing second. Sharing a bedroom was not an option. She clenched her teeth and glared at AJ, trying to signal that they were fighting and not getting along. A couple on the outs wouldn't be forced to stay in the same room.

He gave her a smoldering look, as though he was so hot for her his clothes were singed.

Darn the man. He was having fun with this. Her temper rose. How dare he get her into this situation and now make it worse? If he thought this was a great way to get her into bed he had another think coming. She pursed her lips and crossed her arms over her chest.

"Now, now." Mrs. Cole's blue eyes twinkled. She winked, a mischievous grin on her face. "I may be old, but I remember being young once. You only have five days together. Enjoy your vacation and each other."

So. Not. Good. Emma inhaled but she couldn't get enough oxygen to fill her lungs. Any minute she was going to hyperventilate. Her gaze implored AJ to do something.

"That's generous and sweet of you," AJ said to his grandmother. "But Emma and I don't want to make you uncomfortable."

Finally! Emma nodded, hoping she didn't look like a battery-operated bobblehead. But that was what she felt like trying to get her agreement across to his grandmother.

"You don't have to worry, dears." Mrs. Cole patted AJ's arm. "This is better than you sneaking around at night. Trust me, you won't be fooling anyone. Especially your old grandma. Besides, it's about time this house saw some action."

Heat flooded Emma's face. She wanted the floor to open up so she could disappear. "Please, Mrs. Cole—"

"Lilah. Mrs. Cole was my mother-in-law. Nothing I did was good enough for that woman." She gave Emma's shoulder a squeeze, but the touch did nothing to calm her tap-dancing nerves. "Technology makes keeping in touch easier these days, but long-distance relationships are still difficult. Make the most of your time together."

The woman emphasized the last word.

Together. So not happening. Emma bit her lip.

"This is your room." Lilah stepped through a doorway. She motioned to the wood-paned windows on the opposite wall. "I love the view of the harbor. I used to stand there and watch for AJ's grandfather's boat to come in."

"That's sweet." Or would be if Emma would see past the queen-size four-poster bed covered with a white comforter and fluffy lace trimmed pillows. A romantic bed. A bed for lovers. Not a boss and his employee. The pillow-sized lump in her throat threatened to choke her.

"The room has its own bathroom," Lilah said. "I took the liberty of putting a litter box in there for the cat."

"Thank you." A real smile tugged at the corners of Emma's mouth. She wished she had a grandmother like Lilah. Emma didn't remember hers. "Blossom and I appreciate that."

Lilah peered through the grate. "The cat must be cramped after being stuck in the crate so long."

AJ placed the carrier on the floor, then opened the gate. Blossom dashed out. The ball of orange disappeared under the bed.

"Blossom needs time to adjust to her new surroundings. That's how cats are. Let me show you the room." Lilah pointed out the bathroom, a closet with built-in dresser and fireplace. "You should be comfortable here."

Maybe if on a honeymoon. Goose bumps covered Emma's skin. She rubbed her hands over her arms. The bedroom was oh so romantic, the kind you might find in a quaint B and B. Not the place she wanted to spend the night with AJ. A total stranger.

Emma forced the word *thanks* from her dry mouth. She didn't dare say anything directly to AJ's grandmother and appear rude. The woman had been gracious, kind and… um, progressive.

"We'll be very comfortable, thank you, Grandma." AJ escorted Lilah toward the door. "Charlie will bring up our luggage. We'll get settled, then see you downstairs."

Mischief danced in his grandmother's eyes. She sashayed out the doorway with the grace of a chorus-line dancer. "Don't rush on my part."

The innuendo was clear. The older woman had given them the thumbs-up to have sex before lunch.

Emma bit back a groan. She wanted to be anywhere but here. Her cheeks warmed. Who was she kidding? Her skinned burned like glowing barbecue charcoals.

AJ closed the door. "I—"

"I quit."

His mouth dropped open. He pressed his lips together, then adjusted the cuff of his dress shirt. "You promised Libby you'd take her place."

"As your assistant. Not your…" Emma couldn't say the word aloud. She squeezed the back of her tight neck. "I realize you got caught in some bizarre matchmaking situation out on the porch, and I went along because of Libby, but this is ridiculous. You're a grown man. A billionaire, for goodness' sake. You should be able to handle a scheming woman without resorting to an impossible charade. I don't like lying to your grandmother. I don't see how you can, either. She's so sweet and really cares about you."

"I'm doing this for my grandmother," he said. "If we're not dating, I'm going to have to reject Madison and call Risa on her misguided matchmaking attempt. That's going to make for an awkward time and ruin my grandmother's birthday party."

"No." Emma held up her hands, palms facing him. "This is way beyond what I was asked to do as your personal assistant. Fix it with your family or I walk."

"You don't have to walk. Everything will be okay."

"How so?" Her voice cracked. She didn't appreciate that his voice remained calm. "Your grandmother thinks we're about to make mad passionate love."

"She's...romantic. Indulge her."

Every muscle tightened. Emma glared. "No way. Not going to happen."

"I'm not asking you to have sex with me. Just pretend we're together. We've committed to the ruse. I can't do this without you."

"No one is going to believe we're a couple."

"My grandmother believes. Risa and Madison, too."

Emma bit her lip, unconvinced.

"I'll find a way to make this work so you're not horribly uncomfortable," AJ added. "Please. I need your help."

He sounded sincere. He'd said *please,* emphasizing the word. But something held her back. Okay, a lot of things. "I don't know. I feel really weird about this."

"Me, too." He brushed his hand through his thick hair. "This goes way beyond what a person should ask of someone they met a couple hours ago, but think about Libby. She's your best friend. I know you'd do anything for her or you wouldn't be here now. By Sunday, you and I will be friends, too, and this won't seem as weird then."

Emma eyed him warily. "You and me, friends?"

AJ nodded. "You're the only person who tells me exactly what they're thinking."

"That's not always a good thing."

"No, not always. It's refreshing to be with someone so open and honest," he admitted. "I'll be honest with you. I panicked with Risa and Madison. I got us into this mess, but I need you to get me through it."

Emma felt trapped. No matter what she decided, she would have regrets. Sure, she could walk away, but she'd agreed to help Libby. Emma hadn't spoken up when AJ introduced her as his girlfriend and led his family to believe they were dating. She bore some responsibility here. Not as much as AJ, but some. She took a breath, then another. "You're used to getting what you want."

His easy smile curled her toes. She promptly uncurled them.

"Pretty much." He sounded amused. "I can afford most things, but I like to believe it's because I want only rational things."

"My being your girlfriend is not rational."

"True. That's more of a necessity."

"I'm a raft of cotton in your sea of cashmere."

"I like cotton. Practical and soft. Low maintenance. Perfect for everyday wear."

The slight change in his tone and way he leaned forward to get closer irritated Emma. She pursed her lips, hoping she looked haughty rather than pouty with duck lips. "Flattery will get you nowhere."

"Not flattery. Honesty."

She chewed the inside of her mouth, not wanting to buy his words, but having a difficult time not believing him. "If I do this favor for you, I expect a few things in return."

"What?"

"More vacation time for Libby. She's so dedicated and

devoted to you, she put her job ahead of her health. She needs more balance in her life, not working nonstop."

"I count on Libby."

"She's not much good to you sick or dead."

A beat passed, then another. "Okay, Libby gets more vacation time."

"With no contact from you during that time. That includes texts."

His mouth twisted. "Fine. What else?"

"I would like you to make a large donation to the Portland Paws Rescue Shelter. They need their plumbing replaced so they can reopen. They are a 501(c)(3) nonprofit so your donation will be tax-deductible."

"How much?"

"Fifty thousand dollars."

"You think you're worth that much."

"I have no idea, but you might think I'm worth that much or you wouldn't have introduced me as your girlfriend because you were afraid of another woman."

A sheepish look crossed his face. "Not afraid. Concerned over the consequences of what might happen."

"Afraid."

He opened his mouth, then closed it. "Fine. Contact my CPA today and tell him to have a check delivered."

"Just like that?"

He nodded once.

Billionaire, she remembered. Fifty thousand might seem like a lottery jackpot to her, but AJ lived in a different world. "There's one more thing."

"Money for you?"

"A home for Blossom. You know people. Find her a forever home."

A muscle ticked at his jaw. His lips drew tight. "That's—"

"The last thing I want." She stared down her nose at

him for emphasis, hoping with her glasses she didn't look cross-eyed.

He swore under his breath.

Emma didn't expect him to be happy, but now he knew what being trapped in an awkward position felt like. "If you'd rather not—"

"I'll find the damn cat a home."

"Not any home. A forever home. One that will love Blossom the way she deserves to be loved and take care of her."

"This is going to cost me another fifty grand." He looked at the rumpled bed skirt where Blossom had disappeared. "Maybe more."

"Libby said you made the Forbes 400 this year. You can afford it."

Emma wasn't sure where her bravado came from, but what was he going to do? Fire her?

"Anything else you want?" he asked.

"That's all."

"Nothing for yourself?"

"Helping Libby, the shelter and Blossom is all I want."

AJ studied her, his mouth slanted and his eyes narrowed.

"What?" she asked.

"Nothing." He gaze traveled from her to the empty cat carrier to the bed, then returned to Emma. "You have a deal."

She blew out a puff of air.

He grinned. "You thought I'd say no."

"I was hoping."

"Is this the nanny or the personal assistant or Emma talking?"

"All three." Emma was about to apologize, but realized he'd put her in this situation. If her behavior wasn't quite up to the Rose City Nanny Academy's standards, oh, well, she was doing her best. "Bringing a real girlfriend would have been cheaper."

"True." He looked away, making her wonder what kind of women he dated. Not nannies like her. "But we'll make this work. We don't have a choice."

Emma remembered this was his first time home in a while. "I'm here to make sure your vacation and the birthday party go well. I'll do my best to play your girlfriend, but that doesn't mean I'll be able to pull off the act. I'm still uncomfortable sharing a room with you. Nothing is going to change that."

"I understand and I'm grateful for your going along with this. Who knows, this might be fun."

She made a face.

"Or maybe not," he quipped. "I'll try to come up with another accommodation option, but until then you don't have to share a bed with me. I'm fine sleeping on the floor and you'll have to be flexible about us sharing a room."

The word brought up all kind of images of the two of them being *flexible* together. Unwelcome images that made her want to fan herself. Not good. Having a billionaire she was supposed to take care of end up with a stiff back while planning and hosting a birthday party wouldn't be good, either. "What if someone walks in and sees you sleeping on the floor?"

"I could say you kicked me out of the bed for eating cookies or snoring."

"I'd still hear you snoring if we're sharing a room."

"We'll have to think of something that makes sense."

"I don't think that's possible since none of this makes sense." She thought for a moment, not liking the option coming to her. "We're both adults. We could share the bed if we put a wall of pillows between us. Or one of us can sleep on top of the sheet and the other underneath it."

Amusement gleamed in his eyes. "Excellent idea. You must have experience being someone's pretend girlfriend."

Heat rose up her neck and settled in her face. Tomato-red, no doubt. She didn't like how AJ kept making her blush.

"No," she said. "But I'm a nanny. Sometimes siblings don't want to share a bed or aren't getting along during naptime. I know all the tricks."

"Then this shouldn't be a problem."

"Maybe not for you, but this is way outside my comfort zone. I'm old-fashioned."

"Old-fashioned in what way?"

Emma fought the urge to shrug. She shouldn't have brought this up. "A few ways."

"Let me guess. You don't call men or ask them out. Wait until you're in a committed relationship to have sex. Expect men to pay when you go out."

Oh, boy. Two out of three. Though his definition of a committed relationship might be different from hers. "Yes, yes and no. I'm fine paying or splitting the check. Otherwise dates can get expensive fast and that's not fair."

"While you're my girlfriend, I pick up the tab. I'm sure it'll be a helluva lot cheaper than $50K and finding your cat a home."

"Should be. I don't eat *that* much."

Laughter, deep and rich, wrapped around her like strong, comforting arms. The sense of security and be-longing nearly overwhelmed her. She took a step toward the window.

"We'll make this work, Emma."

"If you say so." Her gaze rested on his smiling lips. Nice lips. She wondered how he tasted. Uh, no, she didn't. "I realize that in public and in front of your family we must act as if we're in a relationship. But any other time…"

"Under any other circumstance, I would never date an employee. We may need to act romantic around my family, but you have nothing to worry about when we're alone."

She stared at the carpet, feeling as appealing as a slice of moldy bread. But she wanted him to leave her alone. If not, she wouldn't be complaining about sharing a room. She lifted her chin and looked straight at him. "Thank you."

"We'll get through this."

The way his voice softened gave her chills. His gaze lingered, practically caressed. Every nerve ending tingled. What was going on?

Not trusting her voice, Emma nodded. She hoped AJ was right about getting through this because she wasn't sure about anything at the moment. Especially herself. And him.

An hour later, with the fake smile he'd perfected for use during interviews and business meetings, AJ sat at the dining room table with his grandmother, his mother, Marianne, Risa, Madison and Emma. His siblings and father would be joining them for dinner.

The reprieve from the entire family would give AJ and Emma much-needed time to practice their couple-ness. Things were not going well, but he wasn't giving up. Visible trouble in paradise would encourage Madison's attention and Grandma's advice, neither welcome.

AJ swung his arm around the back of Emma's chair. A friendly gesture, not the slightest bit intimate. He didn't want his pretend girlfriend joining the cat under the bed.

Emma stiffened, her back ramrod straight. She didn't

glance his way, but scooted forward, putting distance between her back and his hand.

If she didn't loosen up, the gig would be up before dessert. He still couldn't believe she'd agreed to help him out with this enormous favor. He wanted to cut her some slack, but they were on display with his family watching.

He appreciated what she was doing. The way she'd leveraged what she did out of him for others, not herself, impressed him. He hadn't been in this kind of partnership since his early days when he needed venture capital for his start-up. He liked the feeling of having a partner, or rather, in this situation, a partner in crime.

If only she'd stop acting as if she were on a bad first date. The first date part was technically true, but he needed her to act interested. Most women didn't have a problem with that. Then again, Emma wasn't like the women he normally dated. He shouldn't treat her like one of them. He leaned toward her. "Would you like another serving of chicken pot pie, honey?"

Her startled gaze met his. "Um, no thanks. I've had seconds."

Across the table, Madison picked at her quarter-sized portion without eating a bite. "Might as well have thirds. Nannies must use a lot of energy running after kids all day."

Emma nodded.

AJ didn't appreciate Madison's I'm-better-than-you tone. He toyed with the end of Emma's braid. "I appreciate a woman with a healthy appetite and curves. Emma needs her energy for me, not just kids."

The gratitude in her eyes made his pulse increase. His stomach tightened.

"Beeeep. Goal rate met," AJ's watch announced. He blinked and hit the reset button. Normally that only hap-

pened when he'd reached the target range during a cardiac workout. That was odd.

Madison took a bite off her plate.

"I have apple pie for dessert," Grandma announced. "It's AJ's favorite."

"Mine, too," Emma said.

Grandma pushed back in her chair. "Glad to hear it. So many people are into cake pops and cupcakes these days. But pie is down-home goodness. Takes skill to perfect the crust."

His mom's forehead wrinkled. She still looked to be in her early forties except for some silver in her brunette hair and the lines at the corner of her eyes. "I thought you went to the bakery this morning."

"I did, but the baker had to get it right," Grandma stood. "I'm assuming everyone wants a scoop of vanilla ice cream loaded on top?"

Emma nodded. "Please."

"Me, too." Madison inched forward in her chair until she was nearly pressed against the dining room table. "I love pie and ice cream."

His mother stood. "I'll help you serve up dessert."

"Wonderful." Grandma kept her gaze on Emma for some reason. "We'll be back in a flash."

Risa wiped her mouth with her napkin, then stared pointedly at Emma. "A long-distance relationship must be difficult."

"Seattle is a short train ride from Portland," Emma said.

AJ tried not to grimace. He hadn't ridden a train since college. "I have a jet, too."

Emma smiled, seeming to relax for the first time during the meal. "True, but I love the train. Much more cost-efficient than wasting the crew's time and all that fuel jetting me around."

He scooted closer, so close he could smell the citrusy scent of her shampoo. He took another sniff. Better than any expensive perfume. "I know you prefer the train, but the jet's faster. That gives me more time with you."

The lines around Madison's mouth deepened. "I don't get it. Nannies can work anywhere. Why don't you move to Seattle?"

A valid question. AJ tried to come up with a logical explanation why Emma wouldn't be living closer to him.

"I may be moving to Seattle," she said to his surprise. "I recently finished an assignment with a family. I'm currently working temporary babysitting jobs until I figure out what to do next."

"Just say the word and I'll have a moving crew at your apartment to pack up your stuff." He knew this was the perfect opportunity to let Risa and Madison see that the two of them were *serious*. "I have plenty of room at my house."

"I know there's room." Emma didn't miss a beat. Nor did she blush. Progress? He hoped so. "But I'd like to have a secure a job before I make any definite plans."

"You don't have to work," he said.

A wistful expression formed on Madison's face.

"I want to work," Emma said, making him wonder if she ever took the easy way out. Something told him unlikely.

"The offer stands if you change your mind." AJ knew this conversation was nothing more than a show for his sister-in-law and her younger sister. Yet he could rattle off a handful of reasons why a move to Seattle made sense for Emma. Starting with a higher salary due to being in a larger city, living closer to Libby and ending with—not him—the cat.

"Thanks." She looked at Risa and Madison. "Sorry for bringing this up in front of you."

"It's fine," Madison said. "You must have a lot of catching up to do."

"Don't mind us." Risa's sounded genuine. "We're family. It's nice knowing what's going on with AJ beyond what we read on the internet."

"I'm only a phone call, text or email away if you'd like to find out for yourself," he countered.

"True, but so are we," Risa said. "Flynn manages to keep in touch even when he's deployed. The last time he was in Afghanistan, he and Ellis kept in close contact. The kids were always asking when they can Skype with Uncle Flynn. They still ask."

"Flynn's amazing. Always has been. The Cole family's personal superhero."

AJ hadn't meant for his sarcasm to be so thick. He appreciated his brother's service to this country, but AJ didn't get why everyone applauded his brother's enlisting in the military at age seventeen, while AJ's leaving to attend a top university was considered traitorous. Pursuing dreams outside of fishing and boat building should work both ways. Especially since each of Ellis and Risa's children had trust funds to cover their education costs through doctorate degrees.

Madison straightened, her face brightening. "Is Flynn going to be at the birthday party?"

"No," Risa said. "He's off somewhere again. Never know where."

"That's too bad." AJ hadn't spoken with Flynn in…a long time. Ten, no, twelve years. "Libby mailed him an invitation, but he's never been one to RSVP."

Risa pinned him with a stare. "Family shouldn't be required to RSVP."

Silence descended over the table. Even Risa was getting on him now.

"I wonder what's taking so long with the pie. The ice cream's going to melt." Emma scooted back in her chair, breaking the tension in the air. "Let's see if your mom and grandmother need help."

Emma didn't wait for an answer. She headed into the kitchen without a glance back to see if he was following.

He was, nipping at her heels, grateful she'd helped him escape Risa and Madison. He'd forgotten that saying anything against Flynn was forbidden in the family. AJ was in the doghouse before even seeing his father. This was not looking good. If Emma and he couldn't pull off being a happy couple, he'd be worse off than when he left ten years ago. He only hoped his grandmother and her birthday party wouldn't be the ones who suffered.

Chapter Five

After AJ's conference calls and interview had been completed, Emma walked along the shoreline with him at her side. A breeze carried the briny scent of the sea and toyed with the ends of AJ's hair, making him look way too sexy strolling on the rocky beach in his dress shirt, trousers and leather shoes. Temporary bosses and fake boyfriends shouldn't be so utterly attractive.

She should be enjoying this break from his watchful family, but being near him increased her anxiety. The man put her on edge with his constant devising and revising of strategies. She didn't need experience in mergers and acquisitions to know lunch had not gone well. Maybe he was going to fire her for being such a rotten girlfriend. Being fired would be welcomed, appreciated even.

"What do you think so far?" AJ asked.

Walking alone with him on the beach was harder than faking a relationship publicly. He was so focused on success that relaxing was impossible. His family's Victorian stood on a bluff in the distance, a beacon to the Cole men after a day on the sea. "Haley's Bay is lovely, and Lilah's house is spectacular."

"True, but I want to know how you thought lunch went."

Of course he did. AJ was worked up over his family. The dynamics were becoming clearer to her, but she wondered if he truly cared what his family thought of him or if the only thing that mattered to him was his grandmother. He hadn't seemed to put much effort into healing the rifts between them. "Not well. Being a girlfriend doesn't come naturally to me."

"You pulled out a win with the moving to Seattle talk."

"That's because I was telling the truth." The truth mattered. When she was a kid, her mother had dragged her brother back into a convenience store after he'd walked out with a pack of gum in his pocket. He'd been only eight, but their mom had made him apologize and pay for the gum with change from his piggy bank.

Little life lessons like that were all she had left of her family. Every physical reminder of her parents and brother had been destroyed in the house fire. Her memories kept fading so she wrote what she remembered in a journal.

She picked up a shell, then rubbed her fingers over the ridges on the outside. "I talked to Libby about moving to Seattle before she left for New York. She's been after me to move now that I'm no longer working for a family…"

"Your salary will be higher. No state income tax. Several tech companies, including mine, provide employee perks ranging from in-house day care centers to take-home dinners for our employees. If you decide you want to try the business world, you could work in the day care center, be an admin, support the development team. Whatever you wanted to try."

"Libby's suggested I do that." And went as far as typing up and submitting Emma's résumé to the day care manager. Not that a job was guaranteed, or that she would take one if offered. "But I was born and raised in Portland. I've never lived anywhere else. Libby's parents are there. Friends. The nanny agency. Families."

Families Emma had worked for. Families whose children had grown up, moved on and forgotten their nanny. Her chest tightened.

"Move back to Oregon if you don't like Washington."

She shrugged, but the last thing she felt was indifference. She'd left so many things behind over the years— foster families, schools, clients, children. She longed for a time when things would be stable. Hers. If she left…

The rocks gave way to damp sand. She glanced back. A trail of footsteps remained behind her and AJ.

Maybe a change of scenery would be good. Something different. A place to make a new start. Put down roots instead of always feeling transitory. "Did you consider moving back to Haley's Bay after you graduated college?"

"Never." The word burst from AJ's mouth. He rubbed his lips together. "But my situation's different. I felt if I returned I would constantly have to prove myself and live with my family second-guessing me all the time. They don't care what I'm able to do for them, give them. None of that matters. You saw how Risa reacted when we talked about Flynn."

Emma nodded, though Risa hadn't been the only one to react. AJ had been on the defensive, and Emma doubted he realized that. He had set opinions about his family, similar to what he said they had about him. Maybe that was how families acted toward one another after you grew up, though Libby's parents had always been warm and supportive.

"My father will be worse," AJ continued. "Flynn's a hero for leaving. I'm a jerk."

For a man who had enough money to do whatever he wanted, the bitterness seeping into AJ's tone surprised her. But ten years of ignoring issues and not talking could harden the softest of hearts. She never thought she'd feel sorry for AJ Cole, and now she did. He needed to let go, put the past behind him and move on. She hoped he could do that. For his own sake. "You're the oldest, right?"

"Yes. Flynn's third, behind Ellis. Bailey's next, followed by Declan and Camden, the twins, then Grady. He's twenty-two. The youngest."

"What's the age difference between you and Grady?"

"Ten years."

"Your mother must be a patient woman."

"She is. I'm not sure how she managed all of us, though Grandma helped. My dad's only fifty-seven, but he's patriarchal like my grandfather. Never pitched in around the house or changed a diaper. Only yard work—men's work—or tinkering with the cars. Fishing and paying the bills, too."

"That explains it."

"What?"

"The reason your father was…is…upset at you for not following in his footsteps. He, and by his example, your entire family, had expectations about what you, the oldest son, would do with your life."

"That's—" AJ rubbed the back of his neck. "Maybe."

Emma appreciated that he considered the possibility. "Younger siblings don't feel as much pressure. I've seen parents go crazy with everything from elementary school grades to recreational soccer when it comes to their first-born children."

"That makes sense, but it sucks for us oldest."

She smiled. "Depends. The oldest child in the families I've worked for are often overachievers. Intelligent. Mature for their age. Excellent qualities to possess."

"If they don't cave from the pressure."

She grinned. "Well, some have been more neurotic than their younger siblings, but not all."

"So now I'm not only eccentric and insane, but neurotic."

"You said it, not me."

He winked. "You said the first two. The third was implied."

"Implied for children under my care. I'm not your nanny."

"I don't need a nanny, but I do need a girlfriend." He laced his fingers with hers, causing her entire limb to crackle with electricity and tingle so much so she had to remember to breathe. "Time we acted like a real couple."

Every nerve ending stood at attention, buzzing like a broken electrical cable. She glanced around, searching for his motivation to do this. Water. Sand. Rocks. Birds. "No one is around."

"Exactly."

She stared at the horizon, not wanting to meet his gaze. Afraid of…she didn't know what, but AJ made her uncomfortable. His confidence, his strength, his wealth intimidated her. Two people couldn't be more different. "You're not making any sense."

Emma pulled her arm away, but he didn't let go. A rough patch of skin rubbed against one finger. A callus. Not something she would have expected on a computer geek's hands. And then she remembered. He hadn't grown up indoors sitting behind a monitor and keyboard. AJ had the hands of a laborer, a boat builder and fisherman. "Please let go. There's no reason for us to hold hands if no one else is here."

He didn't release her hand and stroked her skin with his thumb. Physical awareness shot through her, sending her pulse rate and temperature climbing. "If you can't be comfortable with me close to you, touching you, we'll never be able to pull this off with an audience."

Darn. She bit on the inside of her cheek, trying to distract herself from the good feelings his touch brought. "Okay, I see your point." Even if she didn't like it.

"So we're good?"

"For now."

She concentrated on her steps. All she needed to do to make this a stellar day was stumble and fall.

"Is this so bad?" he asked.

"No." Her hand snuggled against his larger one, their fingers laced together in a way that felt natural, not awkward. Though she'd die before admitting that. "Holding hands is part of my job description."

He raised an eyebrow.

"As a nanny," she clarified. "Though this is different from the last time I held hands with a guy."

"Should your pretend boyfriend be jealous?"

"Well, Ewan's collection of superhero action figures is to die for," she teased.

AJ's eyes widened. "Action figures? How old is Ewan?"

"Four. Cute as can be, too. Drives all the girls at preschool crazy with his big blue eyes and blond hair. He's going to be a real ladies' man once he outgrows his infatuation with men in tights, masks and capes."

"Sounds like I've got some tough competition." AJ rubbed his chin with his free hand. "But I'd wager my collection of sports cars beats his action figures."

"Depends on if you'll let me drive one or not. Ewan shares his."

"I only have the limo with me."

"Too bad." She liked his sense of humor. Talking with him like this was easy. Fun. "But you've got one thing in your favor."

He winked. "Only one, huh?"

"So far." She bit back a smile, trying to act serious, when all wanted to do was laugh. "Ewan's hands were sticky no matter how many times I asked him to wash them. Yours aren't. That's an improvement."

He swung his arm higher and hers, attached to his hand, followed along. "This is about as kidlike as I get. Unless you count liking saltwater taffy. And that does make your hands sticky if you're not careful."

"Well, if you want to know the truth, sports cars are cooler than action figures."

"I can't imagine being a nanny, or a parent for that matter. Sticky hands, fights and demands. I want results ASAP. You said it talking about my mom. Raising kids takes patience I don't possess. Even a pet who didn't do what I wanted would annoy me."

"I imagine being a CEO is like raising kids times a thousand. Fights and demands among staff. Appeasing stockholders. The constant need to innovate and be efficient. All those employees and budgets, not to mention stockholders."

He glanced off to his left. "Then we're even."

AJ must be kidding. She half laughed. "If you mean we're both human living on this planet, then yes, we're even. Other than that…"

With a tug against her hand, AJ spun Emma around like a ballroom dancer, until she stopped in front of him. He stared down at her with a mischievous gaze.

"What's going on?" she asked.

"If we're really going to sell being a couple, there's something else we need to practice...kissing."

Her heart slammed against her chest. "You want to kiss me now?"

"Practicing holding hands worked. Practicing kissing seems the next logical step."

"There's nothing logical about this." The space between them, less than a foot, buzzed with energy. A strange combination of anticipation and nervousness buzzed through her. "But a kiss would probably make your grandmother happy."

"Exactly. So you're game?"

"For one brief practice kiss, yes."

"That's all I'm asking for."

AJ leaned toward her. Emma met him halfway.

His lips touched hers. *Soft,* that was her first thought. *Warm with a hint of salt* was her second. The taste, not exactly sweet, but yummy.

Her eyelids closed.

Remember, he's not your boyfriend.

The truth was easy to forget. The kiss felt as real as the pebbles beneath her shoes, but much, *much* nicer.

AJ wrapped an arm around her, bringing her closer, bridging what little space separated them. He deepened the kiss. His lips moved over hers, sending pleasurable sensations into places she didn't know existed.

Not real. Logic tried to stop her from feeling oh, so good and desired. *It's pretend. That's the only reason he's kissing you. For practice. Like holding hands.*

But the kiss felt real. Her lips thought the kiss was real. Her body reacted as if this was for real. Too much for a practice kiss. She opened her mouth to tell him that and his tongue slipped into her mouth, taking the action as an invitation to visit, explore, taste, tease.

Oh, wow. She gripped his shirt. A good thing his arm was around her or she might sink to the sand. Her knees turned to taffy, barely supporting her. Triumph, that AJ was into kissing her for more than just practice, mixed with panic, because practice kissing a gorgeous billionaire was a bad idea for her sense of balance. Wow, the man could kiss.

His hand moved up her back, sending another wave of tingles. Her temperature spiraled, matching the desire building within. She arched to deepen the kiss. She wanted more, so much more. If the man hadn't made billions programming social media sites, he would make at least a million with his kisses.

A red light flashed in her mind. Caution, danger. This time, Emma recognized the warning, knew she needed to act.

Stop. Stop. Stop. This time logic wasn't shouting, but common sense. With her heart pounding in her ears, drowning out everything around her, telling her to keep kissing him, she knew that was exactly what she needed to do.

She dragged her mouth away from his, but her lips continued tingling and the rest of her body, as well. The confusion in AJ's eyes matched the way she felt.

"So this is why you went on a walk," a man off to her left yelled across the rocks. "Didn't want to make out at Grandma's."

Another man laughed. "Not too late to book a room at the B and B or inn."

Emma's face, no doubt flushed from kissing, burned hotter. She glanced to the side to see two good-looking, incredibly fit men walking toward her. The kind of hot guys who worked out at those industrial gyms in Portland tossing beer kegs and pushing huge tires. Both men were tall, maybe taller than AJ, and had dark hair like him though different styles. Their casual dress, athletic swagger and curious smiles directed at her and AJ spelled trouble. She remembered his warning and knew who the two must be. "Your brothers."

"Declan and Grady."

"Did you know they were here?"

"No or I wouldn't have let you stop kissing me."

Feminine pride rushed through her. AJ had taken the practice kiss further not for show but because he enjoyed kissing her.

"We may need to practice some more," he said.

For a practice kiss, her reactions hadn't been faked. His kiss had sent her pulse sprinting toward the finish line, her temperature into a feverish zone and her heart rate into ninety-minute Zumba intensity level. Emma needed to dive into the bay to unmuddle her mudkiss-confused head and body. "I think we're good."

One sexy brother with a scruff of whiskers, hair tied back and clear hazel eyes hooked his thumb through a belt loop. "You not only come home for the first time in ten years, but bring a pretty woman. Trying to show us up again, bro?"

Emma liked having a hot guy compliment her, but she remembered AJ's warning about his brother. This one must be a natural-born maneuverer like AJ. She would have to be careful around all the Cole men.

AJ pulled her against him, close enough to hear the sounds of his breathing, uneven like hers. The kiss or nerves? She wouldn't expect him to be worried, but then again with her as his so-called girlfriend, he might be concerned how she would act in front of his brothers. The least she could do was try. She hadn't at lunch. Not really.

Emma placed her hand on his chest, staring at her fingers to keep her gaze from straying to his lips. His heart beat rapidly beneath her palm. She looked up.

AJ's surprised gaze met hers.

She forced a smile. "Aren't you going to introduce me, sweetie?"

The word sounded strange coming from her lips given she wasn't talking about someone under the age of ten, but she didn't allow her smile to falter or her hand to move or her feet to take ten steps back. Because she wanted to do all three. She wanted to run far, far away from Haley's Bay and pretend she'd never heard of the place, because if she didn't run she would want to kiss her pretend boyfriend on the lips again.

"These are two of my brothers, Declan and Grady. This is my girlfriend, Emma." AJ held her possessively, his hand on her waist, making her feel as though she not only was dating him, but also belonged. She liked the unfamiliar feeling very much. "Thought she should meet the family in case it's another ten years until we come back."

Both men's eyes widened. They must have picked up on his use of the word *we,* too. She had to give AJ credit. The man knew what to say to get his point across.

Grady, wearing a navy T-shirt with the words Port of Haley's Bay printed across his chest, stood next to them and touched AJ's shoulder. His eyes were the same green as AJ's, but he had his mother's smile. "Happy you're home. I'd hug you, but you've got your arms full. Not that I blame you. I'd rather hold her than hug me, too."

The men's gazes raked over Emma, making her feel like a fish hanging from the end of a pole with a hook through her cheek. Was she good enough to keep or should they toss her back into the water?

Not that she cared, not much. Being on display wasn't the most comfortable feeling, but more was going on than just her being introduced as their brother's girl. She loosened her hand from AJ's, then slipped her arm around his back. He tensed for a nanosecond before relaxing and pulling her even closer.

"Hello." She worked hard to keep her smile in place. "I'm Emma Markwell."

Declan's scruffy grin widened. "I'm Declan. It's so nice to meet you, Emma."

The charm in his voice matched the curiosity in his gaze. Confidence must be a family trait. Declan oozed self-assurance and sex appeal.

"You're one of the twins," she said.

"That's right," Declan said. "My sister Camden is four minutes and twenty-eight seconds older. You'd think it was forty years. But I can do more pull-ups than her. We're about even with push-ups."

The affection for his twin sister loosened Emma's bunched shoulder muscles. She would never remember all these people. Not without seeing them and putting faces with names. "I'm sure you could do more pull-ups and push-ups than me using only one hand."

Declan sidled up to her, his salt-of-the-earth scent appealing at a gut level. These Cole brothers must drive the women of Haley's Bay crazy. "I'd be happy to help you with your technique. A few lessons and you'd be good to go."

"Back off." AJ's firm voice reminded her of his conference call on the jet. "I warned Emma that you bozos hit on any woman new to Haley's Bay. Remember she's taken."

AJ's jealousy surprised and intrigued her. He had the

boyfriend acting down. Her turn to get in on the action. Emma ran her fingertip along his jawline. "Guess I should have let you put that ring on my finger after all."

He brushed his lips across hers, long enough to make her want more. "Damn straight, but you will."

An image of an engagement ring flashed in her mind. A thrill trembled through her even though she knew AJ wasn't serious.

"Ring, huh?" Declan asked. "Mom mentioned you two might be moving in together, but this takes things to another level."

"And leaves Madison for us." Grady stepped forward. His bright smile and straight white teeth belonged in a toothpaste ad. "So glad you're here, Emma. It's great to see my big brother settling down with a real woman, not some lollipop head with extensive plastic surgery. No offense, bro."

"None taken," AJ said. "Emma is as real as they come."

She wasn't sure what to say. "Thank you, I think."

"It's a compliment," AJ assured her. "And one of the reasons I brought you home. To show them that what they see on tabloids and read on the internet isn't always the truth."

Except in AJ's case, Emma knew he dated actresses, models and socialites. Never for long, much to his dates' chagrin. That was why so many spilled their billionaire dating woes to the media, at least according to Libby. Why have a pity party for one when you could invite everyone in line at the grocery store to join in for a few minutes?

"Mom and Grandma are surprised," Grady said.

"Us, too," Declan admitted. "But in a good way. Dad's reaction will be interesting. Not because of you, Emma, but our father has some preconceived notions about AJ and his life."

"What my brother's trying to say is don't let my father's negativity bother you." AJ's defensive tone returned.

"Dad's…" Declan shook his head. "Who knows how he'll act. Ten years is a long time."

"It'll be fine," Grady said. "Dad's mellowed."

Declan shot his younger brother a sideward glance.

"A little," Grady added.

Tension emanated from AJ. She gave him a half hug. That was what a supportive girlfriend would do. At least she hoped so. "I look forward to meeting him and the entire family."

"The feeling's mutual." A dimple appeared on Grady's left cheek. The guy really was cute. Young, but she wondered if this was how AJ looked when he was in his early twenties. "We never thought AJ would settle down again."

Again? Interesting. Libby had never mentioned a woman from AJ's past, but Emma reminded herself his personal life was none of her business. "Your brother is an amazing man. He goes after what he wants."

"I do, and I have what I want." AJ brushed his lips across her neck, sending tingles zipping through her. The guy seemed to enjoy playing the boyfriend role and taking advantage of their deal in front of his brothers.

"Thank you." She might be a nanny from Portland, Oregon, but his words made Emma feel like the most desirable supermodel in the world. But she resented having him be the one to make her feel that way. If she'd wanted to play house, she could have done that for real with Trey, getting an instant family in the process, but she didn't want to be a fill-in wife for a widower who was lonely and desperate to find a mother for his girls. Not after years spent in the foster system with so many different families.

Someday, Emma would find what she was looking for—a man who loved her unconditionally. She would finally have her own family. Until then she'd bide her time. And as long as she was in Haley's Bay, she'd pretend to be head over heels in love with AJ Cole. But right now she needed a break from the charade. She had a feeling tonight would be harder than lunch and this. "I should check on Blossom."

"I'll go with you," AJ said.

She ran her hand along his arm. "Thanks, but stay here and catch up with your brothers for a few minutes. We'll have plenty of time together."

She didn't wait for an answer, but walked in the opposite direction back toward the Victorian.

"Not your usual type." Declan's voice carried.

Emma slowed her steps to hear AJ's reply, then changed her mind, accelerating as if she were at the start of a 5K race. Whatever AJ said to his brothers didn't matter. His words would be a lie, no more real than their kiss a few minutes ago.

And that bothered her. When he asked what she wanted for herself, she should have said money. The cost of therapy when she returned to Portland or enrollment in a diet center after she overdid the sweets was going to be expensive. But she hadn't. She would have to rely on her nanny skills to keep her wits about her and survive the next five days with AJ Cole.

Chapter Six

"Not your usual type."

Declan's words hung in the air, punctuated by the cry of a seabird overhead. Tension thickened. AJ didn't mind if his taste in women was the issue, but he didn't like the way his brother insinuated something was wrong with Emma. Emma, whose spicy kisses surprised the hell out of AJ and made him want another taste of her. His hands balled. "You haven't seen me in ten years and that's all you have to say?"

"Thought talking about your girlfriend would be better than asking you to buy me a new truck or a house." Declan lifted one shoulder in a casual gesture. "But what the hell do I know? It's not like you haven't been generous with mysterious items showing up in the driveway or unexpected deposits in our bank accounts, but if you're making a list: black, king cab, 4x4, and a three-bedroom, two baths with an ocean view will do. Fenced yard would be good. Someone to scoop up my dog's crap would be nice, too. That gets old."

Declan's humor and wry grin evaporated the tension. AJ would like to do more for his family and had, until a cease and desist letter arrived from the only legal counsel in Haley's Bay, his cousin Tyler, telling AJ his gifts to family members were no longer necessary or welcome. He flexed his fingers. "You're wasting your charm and talents earning a living on the water. You'd be a natural in sales."

"Like I said, what do I know?"

"I'll take a truck and a house, too, if you're playing Santa in August," Grady piped up, the same way he used to do when he was little and trying to be heard.

And like then, AJ ignored the youngest one. Grady would get his turn soon enough. "Good to see you again, Dec."

Declan embraced him, the familiar scent of sweat, salt and fish bringing back a rush of memories. "Been way too long, bro."

A lump lodged in AJ throat, burned like a hot coal. His brother's embrace and warmth were welcome but hurt in a way AJ hadn't expected. Declan was seven years younger, more a shadow and pest than a buddy growing up. Now he was a man. AJ had missed a lot during his exodus. He stepped back, took a hard look at his brother. "You're no longer a scrawny kid."

Declan rocked back on his heels, raised his chin. "Taller than you."

"You are." AJ tried not to feel weird about that. He'd always been the oldest, the smartest, the tallest.

"I'm taller than both of you. And stronger." Grady's chest puffed. His biceps showed beneath the sleeves of his T-shirt. "I can finally kick all of your butts after years of being called the baby. Except Camden's since Dad would kill me if I ever fought a girl."

"Woman," AJ and Declan said at the same time.

"Jinx, you owe me a Coke," Declan teased the way they had when they were kids.

Joking around with his brothers was something AJ missed. Nowadays he was never sure if people were laughing at his jokes because they were funny or because they wanted something from him.

"Being taller and working out can't change your birth order," Declan continued. "You'll always be the baby, even now that Mom and Dad have grandkids."

Grady frowned. "That sucks."

"Live with it," Declan joked. "Though you might earn a little respect now that you're wearing a badge."

"Badge?" AJ asked.

Grady's green eyes twinkled. "Surprise! I told you I had news."

"Not exactly," AJ corrected. "You texted about applying for a new job, but nothing more."

"It's true." Pride filled Declan's voice. "Our baby brother is Haley's Bay's newest police officer."

"One day I'm going to be chief," Grady said with the same enthusiasm he showed on Christmas morning about his gifts from Santa. "Just watch and see."

"When did this happen?" AJ asked.

"Just finished the academy. My degree in criminology helped. Thanks for covering the tuition."

"My part was easy. Congrats." Shaking Grady's hand, AJ wondered what their father thought of this, but didn't want to ruin the moment by bringing up their dad. "Things have changed around here."

"Some things," Declan agreed. "Not others."

AJ wondered which group his father would belong in, most likely the latter. "Well done, Grady."

"Thanks," he said. "So far it's been great. Ladies love

a man in uniform. Especially the tourists. My cell phone contact list is going to be full of pretty women."

"Remember what I told you." Declan motioned to AJ. "Don't settle down with just one. Loose and carefree is the only way to be until you're over thirty and old like AJ."

"Gee, thanks," AJ said.

"Anytime, bro." Declan slapped his arm. "So how long has Emma had you whipped?"

AJ gritted his teeth. That was the last thing he'd been since Natalie broke off their engagement when he was at college and married his friend Craig.

"From the moment we met." Not a lie, because the day they met was the day they started "dating." No one needed to know that was today. "Speaking of Emma, I should get back to the house and see how she's doing."

Maybe AJ could get her to practice another kiss or stage a kiss in front of his family. He still couldn't believe the way she'd kissed him back. He wondered what else he would discover about the nanny.

AJ turned and walked toward the house. His brothers fell in step on either side of him.

"Emma seems nice." Grady scooped up a rock and tossed it into the water. "A little young."

"She's older than you," AJ said. "Twenty-six."

"Still robbing the cradle," Grady teased.

AJ didn't respond.

"Emma's too short to be a model so she must be an actress," Declan said.

"She's a nanny."

Declan made a face. "I thought you only dated actresses and supermodels. That's who you're always pictured with online."

Interesting. His brother had kept up with AJ's private life. He hadn't expected that. Nor thought about doing the same thing in return. "The paparazzi catch me with those dates, but I go out with all kinds of women."

Declan eyed him warily. "You and Emma aren't exclusive, but are talking moving in together?"

"And rings," Grady added. "Sounds weird if you ask me."

Damn. AJ's neck tightened. He needed to be more careful and think like a boyfriend. But he hadn't seriously dated a woman in a very long time.

"We're exclusive. I was talking before I met Emma." Which had only been a few hours ago. Comical almost. Another slipup wouldn't be so funny. "She might not be famous, but she's exactly what I need."

Another woman might use this situation to her advantage, but something about Emma, something that had nothing to do with her friendship with Libby, told AJ he could trust the nanny, even though he trusted few people. He kicked a rock with the toe of his leather shoe.

Emma's willingness to go along with being his girlfriend even though she had doubts showed him she thought of others before herself. A woman who would sell this story to a tabloid would not care about her friend's work schedule or an animal rescue group or a foster cat.

He stopped on the opposite side of the road from their grandmother's house. Cars he didn't recognize were parked in front of the limousine. Noise came from inside the house. He hoped Emma was okay. "Full house."

"Mom was on the phone inviting others when we headed out to find you. I'm not sure she believed you'd really show up." Declan's voice held a bitter edge.

"Don't blame me." Nothing had been worth defying the old man until now. AJ would do anything for his grandmother. "You heard what Dad said about my not coming back unless I planned to take over the business."

"Right," Declan said. "Like you were always so awesome listening to Dad."

"I sure wouldn't have ignored my brother for ten years just because Dad said to."

"Not fair."

"The girls and Grady remained neutral. You could have, too." Losing his oldest brothers had been hard on AJ. "Seattle isn't that far away."

"You can't change the past. Clean slate starting now." Grady stepped off the curb, his cop mediation skills already in use. "Come on. Grandma's probably put out appetizers. I could go for a stuffed mushroom. I'm starving."

He jogged across the street with a bounce to his step.

AJ stepped onto the road. He remembered how his little brother loved to play cops and robbers when he was younger, except Grady wanted to be the bad guy. "He's really a police officer?"

"Hard to believe, I know." Declan shook his head. "Grady always got into so much trouble I figured he'd end up behind bars, but as soon as he showed interest in police work Dad told him to go for it."

AJ's jaw dropped. "That's…"

"Shocked the hell out of me, too. But Dad said fishing isn't for everyone. Especially when Grady would rather be in the water than on a boat."

"Are you talking about our father or some alien being who took over his body?"

"Dad's a tad bit more open-minded these days. You'll see."

AJ wasn't sure he would. Nothing he did had ever been good enough for their father. High grades and test scores hadn't been important. Winning a prestigious science competition had earned him a snicker, not praise. Getting seasick during rough waters brought nothing but scorn.

"I will warn you, though," Declan continued. "Dad still thinks you made a mistake leaving and should return to Haley's Bay."

"Thought he would."

"He can be hardheaded."

"Doesn't matter if his head's made of concrete. My business, my life, is in Seattle."

"Your family is here. I'm not buying it. You could move your business to Bora Bora if you liked. But then again I don't really know you anymore."

Which is why AJ had never been back until now. No one in his family understood who he was or respected his work. Moving a multibillion-dollar corporation was not as easy as buying a nice piece of property on the bluff.

He knew returning was a mistake. The question was how big a mistake would coming back to Haley's Bay for his grandmother turn out to be.

At the house, Emma checked on Blossom, still under the bed, kicked off her shoes and called the two party vendors to set up appointments for tomorrow. She sat on the edge of the bed, grateful for a moment alone.

"Emma, we need your help."

She recognized Lilah's voice, slipped on her shoes and made her way to the kitchen. "What do you need?"

"Be a dear and slice the garlic bread, please," Lilah said. "There are eight loaves."

With a cutting board underneath the first loaf and a serrated knife in hand, Emma stood at the counter and set to work. Music played from the living room. People came in and out of the kitchen, introducing themselves in a flurry of words and busyness.

Two loaves later, a satisfied feeling settled in the center of Emma's chest. She'd never been part of a large family. Both her parents were only children. Libby was an only child until Emma moved in during high school. She'd never cared for more than three children at a time, unless at a party.

She'd wondered what being part of a large family would be like. Today, she was getting a glimpse and loved what she saw.

"Cut a few slices in half for the kids." Marianne, AJ's mother, stirred a huge pot of marinara sauce simmering on the stove. Her brown shoulder-length bob hairstyle suited her casual floral print shirt, jean skirt and sandals. Her arms constantly moved, if not stirring then accentuating her words with her hands or hugging a child who popped into the kitchen. She exuded warmth and friendliness. "They never eat a whole piece. And with all these extra people who showed up we might not have enough."

Lilah tossed a gigantic bowl of fresh baby greens with her homemade poppy-seed dressing. She waved off her daughter-in-law's concern with the tongs. "I've been doing these big dinners for decades. We'll have plenty of food."

"Everything smells delicious." Emma sliced the third loaf, still warm from the oven. AJ's sisters, Bailey and Camden, were in the dining room where dinner would be served buffet-style, the only way to feed a crowd, according to Lilah. Risa and Madison were off having pedicures, but Risa's kids were running around somewhere. Her husband, Ellis, too. "It's nice of you to throw this welcome-home party so people can see AJ."

"Easier to have people over once then having them come each night. Haley's Bay is a wonderful place to live, but like all small towns, people are curious, especially when anything changes."

"AJ's been away a long time."

"True, but they also want to meet you."

The knife slipped and crashed against the cutting board. Emma picked it up, reminding herself to be more careful. "Why me?"

"To see if you're anything like Natalie, his ex-fiancée." Lilah spoke as if she were talking about some girl he'd taken to a homecoming dance, not wanted to marry. "You're not. She was…"

"Mom," Marianne said, her voice rising at the end of what suddenly became a two-syllable word.

"I was just going to say Natalie was impatient, wanting to get married so badly she broke up with AJ to marry Craig Steele. But her loss is your gain."

Emma continued slicing the bread, unsure what to say. She was trying to digest that AJ had been dumped by his fiancée for another man, and also that he'd been engaged. Maybe he wasn't quite the player she thought if he'd been serious enough about a woman to propose. She'd never been close to that herself. Truth was, she rarely dated these days, a combination of her job and wanting quiet time when she wasn't working. The Cole family had a totally false impression of her, thanks to AJ, and the less she said the better.

But she enjoyed being here, surrounded by these loud, happy people. Strangers, yes, but the love they showed each other warmed her heart and reaffirmed what she wanted most of all—a family.

Kids darted in and out, grabbing handfuls of chips from a basket and cans of soda from the refrigerator, laughter bubbling from their lips. Crumbs fell to the floor but no one seemed to mind.

"Don't run with food in your mouth," Marianne shouted after three young boys bolting from the kitchen. She stared lovingly after them, then stirred the sauce with a wooden spoon. "I remember when they couldn't crawl and now they won't sit still. The family keeps getting bigger and older."

"Older and better." Lilah wiped her hands on the front of her Kiss the Chef apron. "Do you have a big family, Emma?"

Her throat tightened with a familiar sense of loss and regret, but her emotions remained under control and no tears stung her eyes. She might not have a family to call her own, but she could live vicariously, even if she didn't belong here. "No, but it's fun to see yours."

Family, as defined by the Coles, included cousins twice removed, neighbors who moved away three years ago and the butcher who provided the Italian sausage for tonight's pasta dinner. A crazy, loud bunch, coming and going like the kids. Emma had no idea where everyone would sit, but Lilah said she had a plan.

The woman might be going on eighty, though she was as sharp and mobile as someone twenty years younger. The contented smile on her lined face spoke of family and love. "I am blessed and very happy you and AJ are here."

A warm and fuzzy sensation cascaded to Emma's toenails. "Me, too."

She meant that, even if she did feel odd misleading them about her relationship with AJ. However she'd gotten here, she was grateful and enjoying herself tonight. "Thank you."

"Yes, thanks, Grandma." The rich sound of AJ's voice sent Emma's pulse skittering. "It's great Emma's getting a chance to meet everyone right away."

Before she could respond, strong arms wrapped around Emma's waist and pulled her against him. She went willingly, reminding herself this display was strictly for show.

The scent of him surrounded her. He smelled so good, better than the chocolate cupcakes Bailey had baked for dessert. Emma forced herself not to take another sniff, even though she wanted one. Going around smelling her boss would not be a smart move, or professional.

His warm breath tickled her neck. Tingles shot down her spine. Real ones like she'd felt when he kissed her. Lips brushed the right side of her cheek. She used every bit of strength not to turn her head so he'd kiss her on the lips.

PDA wasn't her thing, but what was going on had nothing to do with a public display of affection and everything to do with convincing his family she and AJ were seriously dating.

Lilah beamed at her eldest grandson. "Emma's been a big help. Knows her way around a kitchen."

"That's part of her job," AJ said.

The lines around his grandmother's mouth deepened, matching the concern in her eyes. "Cooking for the man you love is a pleasure. You make Emma sound like one of your employees."

AJ's startled gaze flew to Emma's. He opened his mouth to speak, but she cut him off. "One of my responsibilities as a nanny is to cook for the children I care for. That's what AJ meant."

Lilah returned to the salad, seemingly satisfied with Emma's explanation.

Crisis averted, for now.

The Coles were trying to figure out what was going on with her and AJ's relationship. That much was clear. She didn't want his family asking too many questions—ones they couldn't easily answer. That would cause friction and might tip off the charade.

AJ cuddled closer to her. Gratitude or show or a combination of both? Emma didn't want to know, because having him so close felt wonderful. Sensation danced across her skin. She raised the bread knife. "Be careful pulling me too close, I'm armed and dangerous."

"That's true whether you have a weapon in hand or not." AJ nuzzled against her neck, making her inhale sharply. He was one to talk. If she'd been in the process of slicing garlic bread, she would have lost a fingertip. She set the knife on the cutting board.

"I'll take my chances," he added, then kissed her neck again.

Tingles erupted. Heat pulsed through her veins.

Not real. Not real. Not real. Maybe if she kept telling herself the kisses didn't mean anything she could ignore the ways her body reacted to him.

"You really came back." The deep male voice sounded surprised and his words edged with something else, something unwelcoming. "Didn't think you would."

AJ's body tensed, his fingers tightening around her. "I'm throwing Grandma a birthday party, Dad. Couldn't do that from Seattle."

AJ's voice sounded strong, but the underlying hurt was unmistakable. Emma wanted to hold him tight and kiss away his pain. She covered AJ's hands with hers, a sign of her support and solidarity.

A man with tanned, weathered skin and salt-and-pepper hair stood in the kitchen doorway. He was tall like AJ, mid-fifties, and the resemblance between father and son was strong. The man's eyes narrowed, zeroing in on her and AJ's locked hands. "I see you brought company."

"Not company," Lilah said. "His girlfriend."

"Emma, this is Jack Cole, AJ's dad." Marianne's smile no longer seemed natural. "Jack, this is Emma Markwell. She's from Portland."

"I thought AJ lived in Seattle."

"I do," he said. "Emma lives in Portland."

"That makes no sense." The man's expression cast a dark shadow on the playful party atmosphere. "How can you be serious with someone who lives in a different state? Didn't you learn your lesson with Natalie about long-distance relationships?"

AJ inhaled sharply. Emma wanted to shake Mr. Cole for acting the way he was and AJ for letting the rift remain strong after ten years. The two men had no idea how lucky they were to still be able to say hi, whether either wanted to say another word or not. She would give anything for five more minutes with her parents and brother. Words wouldn't be necessary. A hug would mean everything.

"Hello, Mr. Cole." Emma used her cheery voice. The one that worked magic when kids weren't feeling well or parents were stressed. AJ's father had the same intense stare as his son, but Emma couldn't allow herself to be intimidated. She needed to be strong for AJ, as his assistant and his girlfriend. "It's nice to meet you. Did you have a good day out in the water? That's what my mom always said to my dad after a day of fly-fishing in the Metolius River."

"A very good day." He studied her the way his sons had out by the bay. "Do you fish?"

"Not in a very long time." Fishing was something her dad loved to do. The family tagged along. She hadn't gone after his death. "But I enjoy eating fish."

"That keeps us in business." Mr. Cole grinned, the smile transforming his rugged face into a handsome one, much like AJ's. "When I heard AJ brought home a woman, I figured she'd hate fish or be a vegan."

"Not a vegan. I love cheese and burgers. Not to mention whipped cream and milk shakes."

"Then you're staying at the right place. My mother loves

to cook with butter. Warn your arteries. Comfort food is her specialty."

"It is." Lilah shooed her hands at her son. "Now get out of here so we can finish getting dinner on the table."

"I need something first. "Mr. Cole snagged a kiss from Marianne. "Now I can leave you ladies alone."

His wife swatted his bottom. "Have the kids wash their hands."

With a nod, Mr. Cole exited the kitchen.

AJ exhaled. "I suppose not making sense is a step up from being a complete moron."

"Give your dad a chance," Marianne said. "He's trying."

AJ's chin jutted forward. "I'm here, aren't I?"

"Yes, and you should be with your father and brothers, catching up with them." Lilah motioned to the doorway. "Get out there."

"But Emma—"

"I have garlic bread to slice," she said. "Go visit with your family."

AJ didn't move, but kept hold on her. "I want to visit with you."

The man was used to getting what he wanted. Not this time. "We'll see each other during dinner."

Lilah gave him a nudge. "You heard your woman, go. We won't spill any family secrets that will scare her away."

"But those are the ones I want to hear," Emma teased.

AJ made a face. "Grandma…"

"Out." Lilah gave him a shove. "Before I decide I want a *My Little Pony*–themed birthday party."

He gave Emma a don't-make-me-go look. Too bad if he wanted to stay in the kitchen; this was for his own good.

"I'll be fine." She leaned closer as if to nibble on his earlobe. Emma had solved many problems on the playground. The situation between Jack and AJ Cole was more complicated than children not wanting to share the swings or take turns on the slide, but she wouldn't give up without at least trying to help father and son talk, if not reconcile.

"And so will you," she whispered.

Chapter Seven

Four hours later, AJ disentangled himself from Madison in the sunroom, leaving her in the capable hands of Declan and Grady. AJ didn't care which one she ended up with as long as she left *him* alone. What part of his having a serious girlfriend didn't she understand?

He had to admit he'd rather spend time with Madison than his dad. AJ had been upset at Emma for making him leave the kitchen, but his father hadn't said another word to him all evening. At this rate, AJ would survive his time in Haley's Bay without too many battle scars.

He wanted to find Emma, to thank her for making him see that his dad wasn't so scary after all these years. AJ should have known that, but her push had been good for him. He checked the kitchen, living room, backyard and front porch. No sign of her. He pulled out his cell phone and called the number Libby had programmed into his contact list before he left New York. No answer.

The last time he'd seen Emma had been two hours ago. She'd been helping his sisters with the dishes. She could be back in Portland by now. His heart tripped. No, she wouldn't have left, would she? His pulse rate accelerating with his steps, AJ made a beeline for the stairs.

On the second floor, the door to the guest room was ajar. AJ stepped inside. "Emma?"

Something banged near the bed. "Ouch. I'm here."

Relief was palpable, except he didn't see her. Though he noticed a smoke detector sitting on the dresser that hadn't been there before. Guess the nanny brought her own. "Where?"

"Under the bed."

He'd been joking about her joining Blossom. "What are you doing under there?"

"Blossom won't eat."

Dedicated didn't begin to describe Emma. AJ walked into the room. Two panty-hose-clad legs and feet stuck out from underneath the bed. Nice legs. "The cat might not be hungry."

"Cats need to eat regularly. If they go too long without food they can develop fatty liver syndrome." Emma groaned, then scooted farther under the bed. "Come on, Blossom. Stop being a diva kitty and eat."

"Blossom will eat when she's ready."

"I'd feel better if she ate now."

Emma wiggled farther under the bed, sending her skirt up another two inches. He tugged on his now too-tight shirt collar. He was going to have to open a window to cool down the room. "Want help?"

"I don't think you'd fit."

"Probably not." But based on kissing her and holding her, they might fit nicely together. He shook the appealing thought from his head. "I can move the bed."

"Why didn't I think of that?" She scooted backward, the hem of her skirt riding even higher.

Look away. Now.

He moved to the foot of the bed where he didn't have a view that would embarrass Emma. He wished he could blame his leering on one beer too many, but he'd drunk only two and didn't feel the slightest bit buzzed.

Emma stood. She smoothed her skirt back in place, straightened her sweater and adjusted her glasses. "Sounds like the party's still going strong. Why are you up here?"

"I couldn't find you. I called your cell phone, but no answer."

"Sorry. I turned off the ringer before I boarded your jet and forgot to turn it back on after we arrived."

"I need to be able to get in touch with you at all times."

"I'm here now." She grabbed a pad of paper off the nightstand. "What do you need?"

"Excuse me?"

"You called me." She readied her pencil. "You must have wanted something."

You. But he couldn't say that. Nor could he tell her that of all the people in the house, many related to him by blood, she was the only one helping him adjust to being home. Libby and he knew each other better but could never pull this fake dating off. They'd talk work and sync schedules and kissing her would be far too uncomfortable. She would never give him advice because that wasn't her job. Emma didn't know him, but kissing her was a pleasure, her advice was sound.

AJ searched his brain for a task that would make sense. "On the flight you mentioned phone calls that needed to be made."

"Done. When I returned to the house from our walk." She tapped her pencil against the edge of the pad. "I spoke with your CPA about the donation to the shelter, and I've scheduled two meetings for tomorrow. Anything else?"

She was efficient. "No."

"Then let's get Blossom out from under the bed."

Damn. He'd forgotten about the cat. But the dark circles under Emma's eyes told him she needed to sleep, not waste more time cajoling a cat. "Where's the food?"

She pointed to a small stainless steel bowl on the floor. "I took that under the bed with me, but Blossom wasn't interested. She skipped lunch, too. I decided to try dry food instead of canned this time."

"Sounds like the cat is figuring if she holds out she might get something more palatable." He picked up the bowl and shook it once. "Dinner."

"I've tried shaking, calling, sticking the food under the bed. Blossom wouldn't budge."

AJ wasn't about to kowtow to a cat. "Give her a chance."

Less than a minute later, the cat's nose poked out from under the bed skirt. Whiskers twitched.

"I don't believe it," Emma said.

He waved the food in front of the cat's nose, then placed the bowl three feet away to draw out the cat. Time to eat."

Blossom's head appeared. Her wide green-eyed gaze bounced from him to Emma, then back to him. The cat cautiously made her way from under the bed, step by careful step, her eyes never straying from the bowl. She sniffed the contents, then ate.

Emma's mouth formed a perfect *O*. If someone other than the cat had been around, he would have stolen another kiss.

"I've been trying for over an hour to get her to eat," Emma said. "You waltz in here, shake the bowl and call her. Now she's chowing down. I don't get it."

"Why should Blossom eat when she can get your attention and make you crawl under the bed to keep her company?"

"I'm an idiot, and you're a cat whisperer."

"You're compassionate," he countered. "I know nothing about cats, but I know behavior. I have a couple coders who are divas. Brilliant programmers, but that kind of personality needs firm handling. The same as Blossom."

The cat glanced up at hearing her name, then returned to her dinner, as if she hadn't eaten in days. Given her weight and appearance, he knew she was well fed.

"You're welcome to manage Blossom anytime you'd like." Emma touched the top of her head. That must have been what banged against the box spring. "She's got me wrapped around her paw."

He should be so lucky. "Let's hope she doesn't abuse the privilege. Head hurting?"

"It's just a little bump."

"You hit hard. Show me where."

Emma stared up at him, above the rim of her glasses. "You don't have to manage me. I'm as far from a diva as you can get."

"True." Genuineness was part of her appeal, another reason this dating game must be difficult for her. AJ had to bluff through business deals all the time. She was clearly a rookie at deception and that, above all, made him comfortable. "From what I've seen, you're a model team player. A hard worker who pitches in where needed with no concern about herself. Now show me the bump."

"Yes, Coach." She pointed to a spot on the top of her head. "Right here."

He gently touched the spot.

She winced.

AJ pulled his hand away. "Sorry."

"It's okay. Just a little tender."

He brought his hand back, more carefully this time. Her hair, still pulled back in a braid, was soft against his fingertips. "A slight goose egg."

"Told you I'll be fine."

"Ice—"

"Would have your grandmother in here fussing over me."

That wouldn't be so bad. An audience would give them a reason to act like a couple, something they hadn't done much of tonight since they'd been apart. "If it were me or the cat or one of the kids who were running around, you'd be the one fussing."

She shrugged, but the sheepish look on her face told AJ he was correct. The long day seemed to be weighing on Emma. She deserved a little TLC. "Change into your pajamas and I'll get the ice."

"I'll be fine."

"Yes, but ice will help the swelling. You'll feel better." He brushed a strand of hair that had fallen out of her braid off her face. His hand lingered on her soft hair. "Let someone take care of you for once."

"It's not necessary."

"Many things aren't necessary, but we still do them out of respect or desire."

"Or duty." Her face flushed a dark pink. So sweet.

"I've never been great with that one." He was operating off the first two options. If he didn't move away from her now, he would kiss her. He'd promised her they wouldn't touch without an audience. Practicing by the water had been pushing the rules. He couldn't keep that up without being disrespectful. But his feet remained glued to the rug, his gaze locked on hers. Was that longing he glimpsed in her eyes?

Something bumped against his leg. Once, twice. He

looked at the floor. Blossom was squeezing between their feet.

"Still hungry, kitty?" Emma stepped back, breaking the connection between them, and kneeled. The cat nuzzled against her hand. Purred. "She's so content. I've never seen her act like this."

The cat rubbed against his legs, leaving orange fur on his pant leg. He hoped Haley's Bay had a competent dry cleaner, otherwise Charlie would be driving to Long Beach or across the Columbia to Astoria. "She's happy to be in a home. That's all."

AJ should be happy the cat kept him from kissing Emma, but he wasn't. Not really. *That* was a problem. Keeping a firm grip on his libido had always been essential for keeping himself—and his company—out of trouble. "I'll be right back with the ice."

Emma scrubbed her face, flossed, brushed her teeth, put on moisturizer, unbraided her hair and changed into a pair of sleep shorts and a camisole in less than seven minutes. Not quite a record, but she wanted to be under the covers before AJ returned.

She stared at the queen-size bed, knowing she'd have to share it soon. "I can do this."

Blossom jumped onto the bed, circled around a pillow then lay on her back, exposing her tummy for belly rubs. Emma obliged. "Make yourself comfy, why don't you? I hope it's that easy for me."

The cat meowed.

"You like AJ so much you sleep with him."

"I'm not sleeping with the cat."

Emma jumped. Her hand covered her chest. "Don't be all ninja around me."

He closed the door behind him. "I didn't realize I was stealthy."

"My heart's pounding."

"Other women have experienced the same phenomenon around me. My ninja skills had nothing to do with their reaction."

The man was too charming for her own good. Rules and boundaries were in order. "Please knock or announce your presence the next time."

"Will a 'Honey, I'm home' work?"

Having fun and playing around would be easy to do, but self-preservation told her no. "An 'I'm back. Are you decent?' will suffice."

His gaze raked over her, a slow appraisal that sent heat rushing through her veins. "If I was your boyfriend, I'd say you're much better than decent."

"But you're not."

"Right. So I'll just do what you ask next time."

"Thanks." And she'd dream he was her boyfriend.

Something sparked in the air. Emma felt exposed. She crossed her arms over her chest, wishing she'd packed flannel pajamas even though it was summer. Staying in the same room was not going to work. Not at all. Sleep would be impossible with AJ Cole lying beside her. "I—"

"I brought the ice." He held up a Baggie full of ice wrapped in a dish towel, but his intentions didn't look friendly. They looked lethal.

"Well done." Her voice cracked. She tried to remember the last time she felt this way about a man. Umm...never? Forget her aching head. She needed the ice to cool down.

A knock sounded. "How is Emma's head?"

Oh, no. Lilah. Emma's muscles tightened.

"Just a minute," AJ yelled.

That would work for about thirty seconds. "What do we do?" she whispered.

He kicked off his shoes and pointed to the bed.

This was one way to get her into bed without her putting up a fight or a wall of pillows. She hopped under the covers, settling next to Blossom.

AJ followed so he was on his side, facing Emma with Blossom on the pillow to his left. He held the ice pack against Emma's head then twirled a strand of hair with his free hand. "Come in, Grandma."

The door opened. Lilah stood with a glass of water and a container of painkillers. "I thought Emma might need more than ice."

"Thanks," AJ said.

Lilah moved closer to the bed. "How are you, dear?"

"Feeling silly that I hit my head."

"It happens." Lilah's gaze traveled from the messed-up bed coverings to AJ's shoes lying haphazardly on the floor. "I hope my grandson is taking care of you."

"He's making a big fuss out of a little bump."

"Let him fuss. Shows how smitten he is."

Emma liked the word *smitten*. Too bad it didn't have anything to do with AJ's motivations in caring for her. "He spoils me."

"I see that," Lilah said.

"You deserve to be spoiled." AJ kissed her quickly, a brush of his lips across hers. "Taking care of Emma is my favorite job."

Her gaze met his. Time seemed to stop for a moment.

"Where's Emma?" Grady entered the room, a beer in one hand and a cupcake in the other. "I had first aid training at the academy."

Marianne followed. She held up a white bottle of pills.

"I have ibuprofen. Do you think we should call Doc Hunter?"

Lilah clapped her hands together. "Oh, yes, let's call him. He makes house calls. He's also single, in his early thirties. Maybe Bailey or Camden will want to date and marry him."

Grady groaned. He ate the rest of the cupcake and set his beer on the nightstand. "You need to let people find their own dates and spouses, Grandma."

"Some need a little push," Lilah said. "That's all I'm doing. A shove here or a nudge there."

"No doctors needed." Grady stood over Emma. "I've got this under control."

AJ sighed. "You hurt her, I hurt you. Got it?"

Grady nodded, but seemed confused. "Pupils are equal. Do you feel nauseous or weak?"

Emma did, but the feelings had nothing to do with her head. She wasn't used to being the center of attention, but that was nothing compared to having AJ so close. The way he played with her hair and touched her played havoc with her insides. Butterflies revolted in her stomach to the point she thought she might be sick. "I'm—"

"Fine," AJ answered for her. "She has a goose egg, but I got ice. A couple painkillers and a good night's sleep, Emma will be good as new."

Grady winked. "If you let her sleep."

Emma fought the urge to cringe, but she had no doubt color was creeping up her neck.

Marianne clucked her tongue.

Lilah laughed. "They hardly see each other. Sleep will be overrated while they're here."

Emma's cheeks burned. Libby's parents had never discussed sex, let alone joked about it in front of everybody.

Grady looked closer at her head. "There's blood."

AJ moved closer. "I didn't see any. Where?"

"Right here." Grady pointed, both men hovering over her, but Emma couldn't see what they were looking at. "The wound is clotting so no need for stitches. You must have hit hard. What were you doing?"

Emma glanced up at AJ, unsure if he wanted her to tell the truth. She assumed most billionaires' girlfriends wouldn't be crawling under the bed and that might lead to more questions.

"Never mind. I think I know." Grady looked over her with wicked laughter in his eyes. "If you get sick to your stomach or the headache gets worse, go to the hospital. You might have a concussion."

"I didn't hit that hard," she said.

"You still want to be careful." Grady looked at AJ. "If she starts acting different, see a doctor. Wake her up every couple of hours to check for changes in mental status and don't leave her alone for the next day or so."

"I can manage that."

Lilah nodded. "I'll provide backup."

Grady lifted a pocket-size reference book from his pocket and flipped to the back. "Oh, yeah. Avoid the pain meds if you can. They'll mask the intensity of the headache. Call the doctor if it's bad."

"I've got this." AJ caressed Emma's chin with his fingertip. "I'm happy to spend the next twenty-four hours right here."

That wasn't going to happen. Especially when she liked him being so close to her right now. For show, she reminded herself. But that didn't explain the tingles a brush of his hand brought. Or how his playing with the ends of her hair made her feel special. Emma sat up. "The appointments tomorrow…"

AJ placed two fingers against her lips, a gentle touch that made her ache for a kiss. "Let's see how you feel first."

"Looks like we're done here. Emma needs quiet and to rest." Marianne motioned Grady out of the room. "We'll say your good-nights to everyone. They can see you around town and at the birthday party."

"Thanks, Mom," AJ said. "And thanks, Grady. You're going to be a decent cop."

Grady grinned. "Already am."

"Well, good night." Lilah walked toward the door. "We'll leave you two alone. But let me know if you need anything."

Emma held her breath until the door closed, leaving her and AJ alone. She exhaled. Then burst out laughing. "That was…"

"Unbelievable," he finished for her. "At least only three of them came up."

"Grady brought his own refreshments."

"At least they weren't here long." AJ rested his head on his bent arm.

"I feel so silly. It's a little bump on the head. No need for any of you to fuss over me."

"People are worried."

"Not people, your family. That's very nice of them." She relaxed against the pillows. "Their worry is an extension of what they're feeling for you. They seem to link me with your being here, and for that gift they're all grateful. Even your dad."

"I wouldn't go that far."

"It's true." She wasn't going to let this go, even if common sense and a pounding head told her she should. "They care about you, AJ. They really do."

He froze. The only sound was the beating of her heart.

"Everyone was nice to me tonight," she continued. "But

all of them wanted to talk about one thing…you. Your family and friends miss you so much."

"Right. That's why I get only form letters at Christmas and printed birth announcements that find their way to my office when a new family member arrives. Trust me. They do fine without me."

He sounded like a rejected boy. "I understand you're hurt, but did you contact any of them?"

He drew back. "Excuse me?"

"Since you left Haley's Bay, who do you still talk with?"

"Grady. Bailey and Camden. Mom and Grandma. Occasionally Risa. That's pretty much it."

"Why is that?"

"They're the ones who make an effort."

"And how about you?" Emma wasn't challenging him. She wanted to help. AJ didn't seem to have thought this mess through.

"Everyone knows how to reach me."

"You're a billionaire. I can't call your corporate headquarters and be transferred directly to you."

"Ten years ago, I was a kid out of college. I was reachable. Hell, I was desperate for a call."

"I'm guessing so were your brothers and father. I'm sure you had their numbers memorized. You probably still do. Boy, you Cole men seem like a stubborn lot."

AJ smiled. "Determined, is what my grandmother says."

"Fine, so you were all determined not to have a relationship with each other. And you succeeded. But what have you gained?"

AJ didn't say anything. He rolled onto his back and drew a deep breath. "We didn't have anything to talk about. If I stayed, there were conditions I couldn't live with. If I left, I lost their respect. Not only my father, but my three oldest brothers who backed him. There was nothing *to* be gained. It was a no-win situation."

"So you all lost. But it's not permanent, right? They're here. You're here. You can fix this. I'll bet you've fixed much worse."

"Maybe."

She couldn't decipher his voice. She didn't know him, but somehow she felt "in" this. He'd dragged her into this. She'd try to be useful. "When you left town, did you just leave, or were their words exchanged with your brothers?"

"I don't remember."

"I doubt that." The way he huffed was adorable. As a mover and shaker of the tech world she could tell he wasn't used to being called to task. But she respected his willingness to think in a new way. She felt safe because he wasn't going to fire her. He needed her more than she needed him. "What did you say?"

"Not much. I may have said a few things about people who wanted to be stuck in a dead-end town their entire lives. Who wouldn't?"

"You were young, but you need to make nice."

"Huh?"

"Mend bridges, extend the olive branch, whatever other cliché you can think of. You never know what might happen."

"Trying to make nice could make things worse."

"Maybe, but expecting bad things to come from good is no way to live. What have you got to lose?"

"I'm not here for my family. I'm here to plan my grandmother's birthday."

"I'm here to do the planning work. You're here to say yes to the details and pay the bills," she clarified. "But only you can reach out to your family and friends now that you're back in Haley's Bay. You need to do that for their sakes and your own."

"Why should I listen to someone I just met with a bump on her head who could have a concussion?"

"Because it's good advice and I'm guessing if Libby were here she'd say the same thing."

"You and Libby are nothing alike."

"I know I can't fill her shoes—"

"I meant that as a compliment, Emma." He adjusted the ice pack on her head. "Libby is a great personal assistant. The best. But she has never spoken to me the way you have. I appreciate hearing what you have to say. You're the first person besides my mom and grandmother who doesn't hold back."

"That's me." Emma giggled. "Honest to a fault."

His smile was mischievous, intriguing. "I'll give you a pass for today."

"Thanks." She stifled a yawn.

"You're tired."

"A little," she admitted. "Go back to the party. I'll rest."

He set the alarm on his phone. "You heard what Grady said. Can't leave you alone. I need to wake you every two hours."

"You'll be exhausted in the morning."

"So will you. We can both sleep in."

Her eyelids felt heavy. She struggled to keep them open. "I'm supposed to be taking care of you."

"You are. Better than anyone's taken care of me in a long time."

Emma could say the exact same thing about him. Maybe they would come out of this as friends. She snuggled against the pillow. "There's something else I've figured out that's in your favor besides your sports car collection and not having sticky hands."

"What's that?" He covered her with a quilt.

"You're a really nice guy, AJ Cole."

"Thanks, but don't let anyone know." His conspiratorial tone amused her. "It'll ruin people's image of me around here."

"You don't want people to know you're nice?"

"Hell, no. They might expect me back next year."

She laughed. That made her head hurt more. "Heaven forbid you step foot in Haley's Bay again before another decade passes."

"If you knew—"

"I'm figuring it out." She adjusted the ice pack on her head. "When I met your dad, I could imagine how Maria in *The Sound of Music* must have felt the first time she met Captain von Trapp. Talk about intimidating. But you don't have to be the same guy who left here ten years ago."

"I'm not. I didn't have a clue back then."

"And now?"

"You think I'm still clueless."

"What I think doesn't matter, but the past will influence the present without us realizing it."

"That's what you think I'm doing."

"I'm trying to get you to understand if you're doing it or not," she explained. "I didn't know you ten years ago. I've known you for about twelve hours so I have no idea if you are or aren't. Only you know that."

"Do you ever turn off the nurturing nanny part?"

"What are you talking about?"

"That's what I thought." He gave her shoulder a squeeze. "Sleep. You've got two hours then we can talk again."

She couldn't wait.

Chapter Eight

Rays of light streamed through the bedroom window, but AJ didn't need the sun or an alarm clock to wake him this morning. He'd barely slept due to checking Emma every two hours, but it hadn't been a chore. A few minutes of pillow talk, then watching her fall asleep with the moon casting shadows on her pretty face, was worth being tired today.

AJ made multimillion-dollar business decisions daily and turned an idea into a successful company worth billions, but others did everything for him, from handling his bills to cooking his food. He hadn't run an errand, written a check or purchased a gift since his company went public. Even before that, staff members had taken over doing the basic things in his life, things he'd never thought twice about doing himself before. His time had become too valuable to be spent standing in line at the deli or vacuuming his living room rug.

Watching over Emma was a novelty. The feeling of satisfaction had nothing to do with profits and good PR. Maybe he should add an element of service to his charitable foundation's work in addition to writing checks and grants.

He lay on his side, looking at Emma. Her glasses sat on the nightstand. She slept with one arm under the covers and one the outside. Long, wavy strands of brown hair spread across her white pillowcase. A few reached all the way to his.

Earlier her lips had been parted, filling his mind with possibilities. Now the slight curve to her mouth intrigued him. What was she dreaming about? Cats and kids? A man? Maybe him?

Yeah, right. AJ smiled at the truth. His money didn't impress Emma. Nothing about him seemed to impress her except his family. What he'd previously considered his most obvious liability were those who didn't believe in him. Yet Emma seemed to bridge that gap and not choose sides. Impossible.

Still, AJ liked her. Blossom liked Emma, too.

The cat slept between them. She rested her head and one paw on Emma's arm. The cat's tail was against him, but AJ wasn't about to move the feline. Disturbing the cat might wake Emma. He wasn't going to do it. If he were a cat, he would prefer using Emma as a pillow, too.

He gave Blossom a rub, her orange fur soft against his fingers, the way he knew Emma's hair would feel, though hers was longer. He'd given his word about not touching her so he hadn't except for a nudge on the shoulder during the 3:00 a.m. wake-up.

Blossom purred, the sound comforting and surprisingly not unwelcome. Kinda cute. Maybe cats weren't that bad. At least this one.

Emma stirred. She blinked open her eyes, then rolled to face him without disturbing Blossom. "Good morning."

"How's your head feel?" he asked.

"Better." Her smile brightened not only her face, but also the room. "Thanks for waking me up through the night. I'm sorry you had to do that."

"Not a problem." And it wasn't. If an employee or someone he knew were sick or injured, Libby sent flowers, balloons or a fruit arrangement from him without asking. Emma was different. He hadn't wanted to pass her off to someone in his family. Waking up a person every two hours wasn't that hard, and helping Emma was a good way to repay her for what she was doing for him. "Go back to sleep. I'll bring you breakfast."

She carefully moved Blossom's head off her arm, then sat. The covers fell to Emma's waist, giving him a nice view of her bare arms and chest. She wasn't wearing a bra.

He forced his gaze to the cat, who was stretching after having her pillow removed.

Emma looked at the nightstand, picked up her glasses and put them on. "Thanks, but I have meetings at ten and one. I need to get ready."

"Your work ethic impresses me." One more thing to add to the growing list. "But don't push yourself. Reschedule the meetings and rest."

"No way."

"Excuse me?"

"I'm not rescheduling. The party is on Saturday night." She rubbed the top of her head. "I'm fine."

He couldn't believe she'd told him *no way*. Employees never spoke to him like that. Then again, he'd never had a discussion with an employee while in bed and wearing pajamas that outlined beautiful curves.

"The bump's almost gone." She leaned over, her breasts

jiggling and making him forget what they were talking about. "Feel it."

He did, wishing he were feeling something else instead. "You're right. The bump's much smaller this morning.

"Don't sound so disappointed." Her voice held a nanny edge rather than the sex kitten tones he preferred when in bed, but then again this was her job. "I'm not going to be an excuse you use to avoid your family."

"That's not what I'm doing." Avoiding his family hadn't entered AJ's mind. He wanted to spend more time with Emma alone, preferably in bed. Talk about crazy. What were they going to do? Play Words With Friends? Maybe he bumped his head and hadn't realized he was the one with an injury. Nothing else would explain his desire to play hooky from life with her. "You heard what Grady said."

"I did, but I'm okay. Really. You, however, look tired and a little dazed," Emma continued. "Rest while I'm out."

He bolted upright, sending Blossom to her feet. "You're not going to the meetings alone."

"I won't be alone. Charlie can accompany me."

"I'm going."

Her slanted mouth was a new look, but the way her gaze narrowed was familiar. She would let him have it in three...two...one...

"You wouldn't be going if Libby were here. You wouldn't go if your family didn't think I was your girl-friend." She pursed her lips. "I'm still your personal assistant and have a job to do. Let me do it."

He liked when she spoke her mind. "What kind of boyfriend would dump an entire birthday party on your lap? Especially when she hurt her head."

"A typical one. Most guys aren't event planners."

"But my family will think—"

"You said you didn't care what they thought."

AJ didn't want to care what his family thought. He told himself he didn't care, but a part of him still did. A big part, unfortunately. He didn't know why.

"You said you only came back to Haley's Bay for your grandmother."

"I did, but I want my grandmother to know I put some thought into this and didn't leave all the details to Libby and you."

His words didn't ring true. Not to him. No doubt Emma would see right through them. Because until this moment, he'd planned on letting her handle everything while he was here, from the party to his family. He didn't know what had changed or why he was fighting Emma on this. He'd known her for a day, but she'd earned his trust and could make independent decisions.

"You're here," she continued. "That's more than enough for Lilah. Enjoy your vacation. Spend more time with your grandmother and family. Relax."

"I'm going."

Emma toyed with the quilt, her fingers working back and forth along the edge. She didn't look nervous, but something was on her mind.

"What?" he asked.

She released the blanket and stared at Blossom, sleeping at the foot of the bed. "It's...nothing."

The way her eyes clouded told him the opposite. She wanted to say something. "Come on."

"If you want to go to the meetings, go. It's not my place to stop you. You're the boss."

"I am." Except he didn't feel in charge around Emma and that bothered him. Being in Haley's Bay was messing with him. He hoped things would be back to normal today. "We'll formulate our plans for the day over breakfast."

"Okay, but I'm getting dressed first. I'm not used to working in my jammies."

"Me, either. Not sure they'd pass as office chic."

"You could be the trendsetter."

"The company has a casual dress code, but pajamas would be pushing it."

"Even for you?"

"Especially for me. Though if there's ever a day I telecommute, I'll have to make it a PJ day."

"Until you have a video chat to attend."

"Shirt and tie and pajama bottoms." He played along, liking that she was smiling again. "No one would ever know."

"I'm sure telecommuters have lots of 'no one ever knew' stories. Especially before video calls became the rage," she said. "I cared for three children one summer. Their mother liked to have conference calls while taking bubble baths. Claimed the acoustics were better in the master bathroom."

"I never knew acoustics were so important."

"I think she liked the idea of being naked in the tub and no one on the call knowing."

He wouldn't mind seeing Emma naked in a tub. No bubbles required. Water wouldn't even be necessary. He grinned at the image forming in his mind. "I'll have to listen more carefully the next time I'm on a call."

"Don't be too distracted."

"Never. Well, unless I hear splashing."

With a smile, Emma gave a slight shake of her head. "Good thing you don't have to worry about being distracted by me. I'm taking a shower so no splashing."

The thought of her undressing to take a shower was definitely distracting. He hadn't slept with a woman in a while. As in having sex, not for concussion checks or a fake relationship. Something about his "usual type" had lost its appeal. Declan hadn't been far off. AJ was ready for a change, though he'd never have an affair with an employee. A man could dream, though, and Emma…

She crawled out of bed, giving him a full view of her in her pajamas, a camisole and coordinating shorts. No panty hose.

…had the sexiest legs this side of the Cascades. Long, firm, the perfect amount of muscle. Man, she'd look great in a pair of heels and a short cocktail dress. "You're a runner."

Lines creased her forehead. "I jog. Only once or twice a week. I do run after children. That amuses them to no end."

"If you want to jog here, there are trails."

"Thanks, but I didn't think there'd be much downtime so didn't pack my running shoes or clothes." She picked up Blossom from the bed. "I'm going to take her with me in case she needs to use the litter box."

Lucky cat. Though seeing Emma in the shower with water streaming down her body would be wasted on the feline. "I'll see what's going on with my grandmother and touch base with Charlie about the meetings."

"I texted him today's itinerary last night." Emma cradled Blossom like a baby. "Charlie will be here at nine-forty. That gives us an hour and a half to get ready and have breakfast."

Too bad they weren't a real couple because AJ knew exactly how he'd want to fill that time—an hour in bed sans jammies followed by a shower for two. His groin tightened. Now that would be a perfect morning.

Thinking about Emma, dressed or undressed, turned him on and made this faux dating thing work. It was also making him crazy in the presence of her barely clothed, hardworking, likes-to-jog, unpampered body.

What was happening to him? The damn cat wasn't annoying him as much. He brushed his hand through his hair. Once Emma finished in the bathroom, he needed a shower. A cold one.

Emma walked out of the ten o'clock meeting at the party rental place in Astoria, Oregon, with an odd feeling in her gut, one that had nothing to do with the man at her side. Oh, being near AJ brought tingles and knots, butterflies and chills, but those were good feelings. Unexpected, unwelcome, but okay. What she felt now was more…not foreboding, but troubling.

Charlie opened the door. She slid into the limo, feeling more comfortable inside the fancy car than yesterday. The air-conditioning soothed. The coast stayed cool, even during the summer months, but the meeting had sent her blood pressure spiraling and her temperature soaring.

AJ followed her into the car. His bare leg touched hers for a nanosecond. Long enough to make her catch her breath. Blossom's sleeping between them last night had been a blessing. Waking to find herself spooning him would have been as much a nightmare as a pleasure. At least they wouldn't be forced to pretend to be dating here.

The door slammed. A minute later, the limo pulled onto the highway, heading north toward the Columbia River and Haley's Bay, Washington.

AJ leaned back against the seat, then stretched out his legs. He looked liked a guy on vacation in his blue shorts, green-and-white-striped polo shirt and flip-flops. "Tony seems a little laid back. More interested in surfing than the party rental business."

"So laid back he's flat on the sand at the beach." The

last thing she wanted to do was send AJ back into business mode, but this was too important not to deal with now. "We need to find another vendor to supply the tent, tables, chairs and dance floor for the party. Tony seems like a nice guy, but he's going to flake on us come Saturday."

AJ straightened. "We have a signed contract."

"Not everyone treats a contract the same way."

"You didn't mention any concerns during the meeting."

Emma appreciated how AJ let her handle the meeting. He must be a good boss, not one who micromanages his staff.

"I wanted to hear what Tony had to say. I was trying to give him the benefit of the doubt, but what he said increased my worries."

"What worries are those?"

"I researched the vendors Libby selected, and checked the most recent reviews. Tony's parents retired. He took over their business a week after Libby negotiated the contract with his father," Emma explained. "Tony's been a no-show for events five times in the past month. Your grandmother's party is the only thing listed on the upcoming event whiteboard. And his phone didn't ring once while we were there."

"I hadn't noticed."

"Libby gave me a list of things to look for with vendors. She's more experienced with event planning and knows what can go wrong. That's why she wanted me to meet with each in person." Emma might not have taken on a party of this scale, but she trusted her instincts. "I'm concerned we're going to find ourselves scrambling if Tony doesn't show up the day of the party. That's why I suggest we hire another vendor. You'll lose your deposit with Tony's company, but have peace of mind of knowing we'll have the supplies we need the day of the party."

"Sounds like a good plan. I don't want anything to go wrong with the party. Do you have someone else in mind to hire?"

Emma nodded. "Libby spoke with four different vendors before deciding on Tony's parents. I have the names and numbers. She did her homework, and until the change in management, made the right choice, especially since Tony's parents know Lilah. I'll find out if her second choice is available."

"Call now." AJ smoothly launched into CEO mode, and she noticed the change in his expression. Hard. A little ruthless. Nothing like the guy she'd woken up with a couple hours ago, who sang her 'NSync songs every two hours to keep her upbeat about the concussion checks. "They can email the contract. I've got a hot spot and wireless printer here in the car."

"That's convenient."

"Some issues are time sensitive. I need to work on the road."

"No wonder you need a vacation. But it's still hard to turn off the CEO, isn't it?"

He shifted positions. "Sometimes, but I'm trying."

Harder than tough decisions to make and firing people must pressure AJ to always be "on." He needed to be the smartest one in the room, the director of the action. His following her to the meeting, that was about her ridiculous twenty-four-hour watch, nothing else. Other than attending, he deferred to her. That made her warm with pride. Emma pulled out her notebook and cell phone. She made the phone call.

Ten minutes later, she gave another party rental place AJ's credit card number, then disconnected. "All set. Contract is being emailed. I'll have Charlie drive me up there later to drop it off so I can meet them."

"Charlie will drive us there."

She knew better than to argue the point. "Fine."

"We have nearly two hours until the one o'clock appointment. Time for some R & R."

"You deserve it," she said.

"Not for me. You."

"I don't understand."

"It's time for you to see Haley's Bay. We can have lunch and walk around town." He flashed her the same charming grin she'd woken up to this morning and made her heart bump. "What do you say?"

Spending more time with AJ without working on the party wasn't the smartest move. But they did have time, and she wanted to see the town. This was also one way to make sure he relaxed. "Sounds great."

The limo pulled to a stop in the harbor's small parking lot. Charlie opened the door, but AJ was the one who took her hand to help her out of the car. "Ready to see Haley's Bay?"

"Yes."

Emma knew he disliked his hometown, no doubt blaming the conflict with his dad and what happened with his ex-fiancée. But AJ didn't look miserable here. He'd smiled last night. He was smiling now. Maybe she'd been correct. Maybe he was letting the past interfere too much. Hating Haley's Bay could be his defense mechanism.

"Anything in particular you don't want to miss?" he asked.

"The candy store. Your sister Bailey told me they have the best saltwater taffy around."

"Taffy equals sticky hands."

"I have wet wipes in my tote bag."

"Then I'll have some, too." He held her hand. "Not sticky now."

She looked down at her hand in his. "What...?"

"This is a small town. My brother is a cop. My dad and brothers might have come in early. Who knows what my two sisters are up to. Not to mention my mom, grand-mother, cousins and friends."

The charade. She'd forgotten for a moment and thought he was really holding her hand. Silly.

"Okay." Emma didn't mind. She liked holding his hands. More than she should. She also liked kissing but that was a little too real. "Let me put on my pretend girl-friend persona."

Maybe if she kept her self separate from the role-playing, things would be easier to handle and not so con-fusing, especially the kissing part.

He squeezed her hand. "I'm ready to be the perfect fake boyfriend."

The longing in her heart for a relationship with a real boyfriend nearly overwhelmed her. Visions of candlelit dinners and making out on a bench by the water swam be-fore her eyes. Where had that come from? Her dates had always trended toward the pizza-and-bowling combo, and the nice-but-not-memorable category. Emma pasted on a smile and tilted her head toward the line of shops across the street. "Let's explore Haley's Bay."

An hour later, AJ held open the door of the seafood café where he and Emma had eaten lunch—salmon coated in a rice flour batter and waffle-cut French fries. Not the fish and chips he'd grown up eating, but tasty. The best part of the lunch, though, had been talking with Emma. She was closemouthed about her life before meeting Libby but he knew Emma had had a far rougher beginning than him, and was drawn to Haley's Bay for its picturesque beauty and curb appeal.

"Admit it," Emma said on the way out the door. "This town isn't purgatory on earth."

Compared to whatever she'd faced that put her into the foster care system, Haley's Bay must seem perfect. AJ knew better—small towns were not judgment-free zones—but he didn't care enough to correct her because he couldn't stop smiling. She made him, in a word, *happy,* a way he wasn't used to feeling. Oh, he was content. He had a good life, but *happy?* That wasn't a word he'd use to describe himself.

But he was having his best day in forever. Better than his last merger. Better than his last million-dollar fundraiser. Funny considering the most exciting thing they'd done was have a souped-up seafood combo and fire a lazy party guy who reinforced AJ's belief that inheriting a company made you less invested than if you'd been a founder.

He joined Emma on the wood-slatted sidewalk. The sun was high in the blue sky. A nice wind off the water turned the weather vanes on top of shops. "I may have exaggerated."

She peered into the window of the souvenir shop next door. "If this is purgatory, I'm in."

"You didn't grow up here."

"I wish I had. Especially now that I know you give full-ride scholarships to any honor roll student who gets accepted into a four-year university. That's so generous of you. Obviously all the people who came to the table are grateful."

"I have a foundation. The money needs to be given away. Kids who live in towns like this don't always have the means to attend college."

She turned away from the display of seashells, beach towels and sun hats. "Kids like you."

Her gaze pierced deep inside him, as if she could see

straight to his soul. He looked away. "I earned a full ride. If I hadn't, I'd have wound up at the local two-year college or not gone at all. I don't want others to find themselves in the same position."

The soft smile on her face filled him with warmth. She pointed to his heart. "This town will always be a part of you. Right here. Welcome home, Atticus Jackson Cole."

His throat tightened. Something about this woman made him feel things he'd either forgotten or never known. He was a computer programmer. Code, he understood. Logic ruled his world. Emotion played a minor role, except, as Emma discovered, when it came to Haley's Bay and his family.

AJ didn't understand. How could she read him when he was so practiced in not giving his thoughts away? Her ability bothered him, left him feeling exposed. He knew exactly what would soothe him. "The candy shop is up ahead. Let's try some of that taffy Bailey told you about."

He opened the door for Emma then followed her inside. A counter with a glass display case of chocolates and other candies was on the left hand side. On the opposite wall, a built-in shelf unit held clear buckets full of different flavored saltwater taffy. A popcorn popper and cotton candy machine sat in the rear of the shop.

Emma glanced at the delicious looking chocolates. "The smell alone is going to add three inches to my hips, but what's that saying? You only live once. Who knows if I'll ever be back? Might as well take home a few souvenirs."

"Choose whatever you want," he said. "My treat."

"Not to scare you, but I have a huge sweet tooth."

"Huge I can afford. Ginormous I might have to limit you."

She smiled.

He smiled back, feeling a comfortable connection with her once again.

"Welcome to the Candy Cave," a familiar-sounding voice said from behind swinging doors. A woman appeared in a white shirt, white pants and pink apron. Blond hair was pulled back into a bun and covered with a hairnet. "I was in the back checking a fresh batch of fudge. Would you like a sample?"

"I'd love a taste," Emma said. "Thanks."

AJ did a double take. No, it couldn't be her. He blinked then took another look. His muscles bunched. He used to think Natalie Farmer, captain of the cheer squad and homecoming queen, was beautiful with her soulful brown eyes, ivory complexion and long blond hair. But her eyes looked tired and weary. Her features were tight, almost pinched, and her ruddy skin made her look older than thirty-four. "Natalie?"

The woman froze. Color drained from her face. Her mouth gaped. "AJ. You're back."

He nodded, not trusting his voice. He hadn't seen her since Christmas break of his freshman year of college. By the time he returned in June, she'd married Craig Steele, one of AJ's best friends. He waited for the anger over their betrayal to hit.

"Hello." Emma greeted Natalie warmly. "I'm Emma Markwell."

Natalie's narrowed gaze flew to AJ. "A friend of yours?"

"My girlfriend." The words came naturally. He wasn't upset. He didn't feel anything for the woman who broke his heart. No emotion, no attraction, no regrets. A shocking but sweet surprise. "Emma, this is Natalie. We went to high school together."

"Nice to meet you," Emma said.

Ignoring her, Natalie's lips thinned. "Has your billionaire brain forgotten we were more than high school class-mates?"

"Natalie and I were once engaged, but she married someone else," AJ said, amazed by his indifference. "How is Craig doing?"

"I wouldn't know. We've been separated since June. That's why I'm working here. But our kids tell me he's doing well." Natalie's eyes gleamed. "He's met someone else."

Emma shifted her weight between her feet, then dragged her teeth over her lower lip. "I'm going to look at the taffy."

She moved to the wall of buckets on the right side of the store. Far enough to give him and Natalie a little space, but the store wasn't large enough to provide much privacy. Emma playing the gracious employee irritated him. She shouldn't have moved away, but stayed next to him acting like the upset, affronted girlfriend.

Natalie cleared her throat. She waited with an expectant look on her face.

AJ didn't know what he was supposed to say. "I'm sorry, Nat."

"Me, too." She glanced over at Emma. "Your girlfriend seems nice."

"She is."

"Young."

He knew Emma could hear every word. "Yes."

"I don't see a ring."

Natalie sounded harsh, bitter. The bouncy girl who floated through life like a princess on a parade float had completely disappeared. Maybe she hadn't really been that way. "Like you said, she's young. No rush."

"I shouldn't have rushed. I should have waited. I'm… sorry. If I could do it all over again—"

"It's in the past, Nat. There aren't any do-overs."

"What about second chances?" Natalie asked.

He couldn't believe she wanted to rekindle their romance. "It's been a long time since we knew each other."

"We were in love once," she said in a low voice. "Who knows what might happen this time?"

He knew, because he might have been in love with her, but she hadn't been in love with him. A woman in love and wearing a man's engagement ring wouldn't have started dating others because she was lonely. Natalie hadn't left AJ for another man. She'd been in love with getting married and AJ had fit the groom mold until his going away to school threatened her timetable. Nat's solution? Replace the groom.

To think he'd let her haunt him for so long. Stupid.

What I think doesn't matter, but the past will influence the present without us realizing it.

Emma was right again. She could teach Mary Poppins a thing or two. He bit back a smile. "I can't."

Natalie inclined her head toward the taffy display. "Because of her."

Holding a paper bag, Emma studied the labels on the buckets of taffy. AJ knew the difference between the two women in that instant. Emma seemed to like the person he was while Natalie had liked the person she wanted him to be. A big freaking difference. She'd made her choices, but AJ felt sorry for Natalie. "I hope things work out with you and Craig."

For their kids' sake, AJ thought to himself.

Executives and employees at his company had gone through divorce. He wouldn't wish that pain on anyone, including Natalie and Craig.

"Thanks, you never know what might happen." Natalie sighed. "Emma's a lucky woman."

"I'm the lucky one."

And he was. In a pretend relationship or a real one, Emma would go out of her way to help a friend or a stranger. She would never break her word or promise the way Natalie had.

Time to put this chapter of his life behind him and move on. He had one person to thank for that—Emma.

Chapter Nine

"The florist is a five-minute walk from here."

"We have fifteen minutes until our appointment. Plenty of time. I want to tell you an idea I had about Lilah's party theme," Emma said to AJ, walking next to him toward the harbor. He didn't look upset from seeing his ex. If anything, he looked satisfied, with a smile on his face and a bounce to his step. That seemed an odd reaction to bumping into the woman who supposedly broke his heart. Declan had implied Natalie had been part of the reason AJ avoided town. If so, that particular concern seemed to have been laid to rest. Very strange.

"Have you tried a piece of taffy yet?" AJ asked.

She carried a small bag from the Candy Cave, but she didn't feel like munching on the taffy they'd purchased. "No, I'm still full from lunch. Would you like one?"

"Later."

Questions about Natalie Steele rattled around Emma's

brain. The woman was pretty, tall and model thin, exactly the kind of woman a man like AJ would date. Though Natalie didn't seem to be living a happily ever after in Haley's Bay. Emma respected AJ for stuffing cash into the tip jar while Natalie rang up their candy purchase. The nickname Attila didn't fit him at all.

Tourists crowded the sidewalk, forcing her to separate from AJ. She let a woman pushing a double stroller pass. He waited for Emma to catch up to him. "You're about to chew your bottom lip to pieces. What's on your mind?"

She ran her tongue across her lower lip. Oops, he was right. Except... "Your personal life is none of my business."

"That's never stopped you before."

"You don't sound upset about that."

"I'm not." He shortened his stride to match hers. "So spill."

She laughed at the term. "I don't have anything to, um, *spill*."

"But you have questions. I'm assuming they're about Nat."

"Yes." Meeting Natalie hadn't made Emma feel inadequate—nothing she could do about her average height and being a little curvy—but seeing the woman with AJ put the relationship charade into much-needed perspective. Time to put a blaring, neon-colored emphasis on the *pretend* part of being AJ's fake girlfriend. When Emma was with him, talking to him as though they'd known each other forever, pretending slipped her mind. She couldn't let that happen again. *Not real.* She needed the words tattooed as a reminder. "Seeing Natalie like that was unexpected. Are you okay?" Emma asked finally.

"Yes."

"Are you going to see her again?"

"What?"

No. No. No. She hadn't meant to ask that question even if she was dying to know the answer. "It's just...Natalie mentioned being separated from her husband. If you still have feelings for her—"

"I don't."

"You were engaged."

"A long time ago. I was eighteen. Young. Stupid. In love. Bought into the fairy tale."

Emma's relief was palpable, something she didn't understand. "And now?"

"Even if I was interested in her, which I'm not, Natalie's separated from her husband, not divorced. I don't mess around with married women."

"Another rule, like how you don't fool around with employees."

A beat passed. Then another. "Not a rule per se, but common sense to avoid complications, lawsuits and jealous estranged husbands."

"That makes sense."

"Glad you think so." Amusement danced in his eyes. "By the way, you were right."

"What about?"

"Letting the past influence the present. I thought I was still upset at Natalie, but once I saw her I realized I wasn't. If anything, I felt sorry for her. Things turned out for the best, even if I didn't think so at the time."

"That's great. I'm glad you bumped into her."

"Me, too. I never thought I'd be saying that."

A tall man caught her eye. Jack Cole stood across the street from the harbor, his eyes locked on her and AJ. The hard set of Jack's jaw and thinned lips reminded her of a sculpture. No warmth or life in the etched stone. "Now all you need to do is work through things with your father."

AJ slowed his pace. "That's not going to happen."

"You didn't become the man you are by giving up."

"Giving up implies I want something from my father. I don't. Not anymore. Just like Natalie. Over it."

"Hmm. Well, that's good to know. Then again, your father's standing at the end of the block. Perhaps you could test how much you don't care by asking his opinion on your last business venture. Unless seeing your dad right after Natalie—"

AJ kissed Emma on the lips. Hard. A kiss full of longing and desire.

Awareness thrummed through her body. Everything on her mind disappeared. All she could think about was AJ. All she could feel was his mouth moving against hers. Fireworks exploded inside her, but she didn't think twice about getting burned. She arched against him, wanting to be closer.

His kisses were like oxygen, necessary for life. She pressed harder against his lips. More, she wanted more. He pulled away from her, ending the kiss, leaving Emma gasping for a breath of air and not sure what had just happened.

"I told you I'm fine." He waved to his dad with his free hand. "Never been better."

That made one of them. Emma blinked, took in her surroundings, forced herself to breathe. She was in big trouble.

Forget pretend kisses. That one had been real. Who was she kidding? They'd all been real to her, even the practice one by the water.

Uh-oh. She wiped her mouth, as if she could wipe away the tingles and the memory of his kiss.

"Come on. We have a couple minutes before our meeting." AJ pulled on her arm. "I'm not interested in your experiment, but let's see what my dad wants."

Emma followed, her actions more robotic than human. Confusion made her brain feel like mush, the same way AJ's kisses turned her insides to goo. She noticed the frown on Mr. Cole's face. "He doesn't look happy."

"That's his here-comes-AJ face." He didn't let go of her hand; if anything, he held on tighter. "Hey, Dad. What's going on?"

"Tony Mannion called me. Says you canceled the rental agreement for your grandmother's birthday."

Emma released AJ's hand and stepped forward. "I'm the one who wanted to hire a new vendor, Mr. Cole."

"I agreed with Emma." AJ stood next to her, put his arm around her shoulder and drew her against him. "It was the right decision."

"We've been friends with the Mannion family for years." Mr. Cole's cheeks reddened. "Hell, I taught Tony how to fish. Call him back and tell him you made a mistake before his parents find out."

"No," AJ said.

Emma slipped her arm around his waist in support. AJ's ignoring his dad's opinion would only make things worse. She tried to send relaxing, peacemaking vibes by rubbing her fingers up his spine, but his back was stiff and proud due to his father, magic fingers or not.

Mr. Cole blinked. "What did you say?"

"I'm not going to do that." AJ's voice sounded strong, but not defensive. "Grandma's birthday is too important to leave anything up to chance."

Mr. Cole's nostrils flared. "His parents—"

"Are RVing their way through British Columbia." The way AJ squared his shoulders. He was in this fight to win, but Emma hated that she was the one who caused the argument. "I doubt they have any idea Tony is ruining the business they built over the years. Not that it matters since you never listen to me."

Jack Cole looked at her. "Do you know what's going on?"

She nodded. "Since Tony's parents turned over the business to him, he's been a no-show at several events. The recent reviews from customers are all negative. Meeting with him this morning confirmed my fears so I suggested we hire another vendor."

"Who'd you go with?"

"A company in Long Beach," she answered.

"Guy Schrader?"

"Yes. We're dropping the contract off this afternoon."

The lines on Mr. Cole's face relaxed. He rocked back on his heels. "Known Guy for years. Good choice. He won't let you down. Good catch on Tony. I'll see if I can get in touch with his parents and set things right there." Mr. Cole glanced at his wristwatch. "I need to get back to the boat. See you at Bailey's tonight for dinner."

With that, he turned and crossed the street, making traffic stop for him, as if Jack Cole owned the town.

"He's a little…gruff," she said.

AJ barked out a laugh. "That's one way to put it. But don't let my father get to you."

"I won't."

"Good." He stared down at her with tenderness in his eyes. "It may be hard for your optimistic view on life to handle, but people don't change."

"I wouldn't say that." Emma had seen the physical similarities between the two men last night, but they shared many of the same personality traits, too. She wondered if AJ knew he was as stubborn, or that she was no optimist, but now wasn't the time to bring any of that up. "He agreed with the new vendor."

"Your new vendor, not mine."

"He doesn't know which one of us picked Guy Schrader. Your dad would assume it was you, not me."

"Maybe."

"Not maybe." She raised his hand and kissed the top of it. "You let go of the anger over Natalie. It felt great, right? Imagine how light you'd feel if you let go of this battle with your dad. Called a truce. You'd float. I'd have to hold on to make sure you wouldn't sail away on me."

AJ touched her face. "Total nutty-in-the-head optimist. If you were an analyst, I'd have to fire you for all the money you'd lose. But in a nanny—I like it."

"I can't be a pessimist. I work with kids," she said with a smile. "I'm supposed to be teaching them, but the truth is I learn so much from them. They get over hurts in five minutes, and make up after fights that same day."

His grin made her think of kids, her kids, ones with his clear green eyes and bright smile. Like her brother, the last time they'd been happy together. A child with AJ would bring that kind of joy back to her life. A family, her own people to love forever. She swallowed, wanting the images erased from her mind. Her brother was gone, soon AJ and his family would be gone, and she'd be alone as she'd been since the fire. Like living with Libby for her last three years of school, this was temporary. Not real. A fantasy.

"We'd better get to the florist." He held on to her hand again. "Did you hear me mention we're expected at Bailey's tonight?"

"Another family dinner?"

"Immediate family only. Bailey's house isn't big enough to hold aunts, uncles and cousins, too."

That sounded like the best kind of problem to have—

too many family members to fit in your house. Although acting the part of AJ's besotted girlfriend wasn't too bad a problem to have, either. Pretending had transformed into an absolute pleasure today. She just had to remember what was real and what wasn't.

"So what was your idea for a party theme?" AJ asked.

"Welcome to the house that AJ bought."

"Very funny, sis." Following Emma into the house, AJ handed Bailey the bouquet of flowers Emma had picked out after their meeting with the florist. The bright-colored flowers would go well with his sister's little cottage surrounded by a white picket fence and flowers growing in pots and containers and even the basket of an old rusted bicycle. "These are for you."

"They are lovely." Bailey sniffed the blossoms, her long ringlet-curled copper hair falling across her face. "Thank you, Emma."

"They're from AJ," she corrected.

"You must be a good influence, because I can't remember the last time AJ bought something on his own," Bailey teased with a smile that reminded him of Grandma.

AJ looked around. "Nice place."

"I have you to thank for that." Bailey kissed his cheek. "I know you thought I was crazy for wanting this foreclosure."

"I'm impressed. You've done an incredible job remodeling." He pointed to a painted textile hanging on the wall. "I like that."

Bailey nodded, sending long earrings clinking against the necklaces she wore. "Thanks. I'm still trying to decide if more blue is needed."

"Looks good to me," he said.

"Says my big brother who thinks anything I make is

brilliant and finds computer code sexy." Bailey gave him a hug. "But thank you. And just so you know, you're not allowed to buy it."

Emma looked around at the artwork covering the brightly painted walls and built-in shelves. "You created all of this?"

"Guilty as charged." Bailey looked at her pieces the way a mother stared at her children. "AJ convinced me I was wasting my talents as a short-order cook and should pursue art instead."

"Art's been my sister's passion for as long as I remember. When she was little, she'd paint rocks and seashells and sell them to tourists," he added, so proud of what Bailey had accomplished. "She made a great omelet, but her heart was in the studio, not the kitchen."

"I still make a great omelet," Bailey joked. "And my rocks and shells are for sale at the souvenir shop. But I'm much happier as an artist than I ever was as a cook."

"Well, whatever you're making in the kitchen smells delicious. It's obvious you have many talents and gifts." Sincerity rang clear in Emma's compliment. The wide smile on Bailey's face told AJ that his sister heard it, too. "I'm really impressed."

"Thanks." Bailey spun toward the other wall, where a metallic sculpture sat, sending her flowing skirt outward and the bangles on her arms clanking against one another. She'd always dressed bohemian-style, even when she was a little girl. "That's my newest creation. I rotate items between a gallery at the Broughton Inn here in Haley's Bay and one in Seattle. But a piece's first stop is my house. I want to make sure each work gets the thumbs-up from my brother's discriminating eyes. As you know AJ's into art."

"I didn't know that." Emma's eyes widened. She must have realized her lapse. "I mean…"

Standing behind Emma, AJ wrapped his arms around her. He placed his cheek against hers. "What Emma means is when we're together the last thing on our minds is hanging out in an art gallery."

"I don't blame you." Bailey sounded wistful. She hadn't had much luck in the romance department, but wouldn't go into details. "Long-distance dating must be tough."

He nodded. "But worth it."

Emma looked up at him through a half moon of thick dark eyelashes. "Definitely."

His heart bumped. What was going on? He tried to let go, but doing so was taking so much effort. His body seemed on autopilot, ignoring captain's orders and drawing closer to the sea nymph. His fingers cupped her hips from behind as though they were beckoned and possessive. She swayed, warm under his touch, and he imagined the skin under the skirt. Lifting the skirt.

He jerked away, such an idiot. Emma was not going to lift her skirt for a temporary boyfriend. And AJ was not going to lift the skirt of a temporary employee, despite luscious hips and their warm sway and his idiocy.

"Next time you're in Seattle, make him take you to his art gallery," Bailey said, glancing oddly at AJ, likely noticing his jerking away from Emma as though the woman had whacked him with a hot poker.

He gave his sister a weak smile. He'd never felt so foolish in his life. Emma's body held him captive.

Her smile looked forced, as well. "I, um, will."

Pretending was getting harder, not easier. He hated putting Emma through this. Only a couple more days… "Where is everyone?"

"Backyard." Bailey led them past the dining room, into the small kitchen where the delicious aromas made his hungry mouth water, toward the open back door. "Not enough space in here. Fortunately Mother Nature cooperated. Ellis, Risa, the kids and Madison arrived a few minutes ago. Grady should be here shortly with Camden."

Emma touched the white-tiled backsplash. "You have a lovely home."

"Thanks. I dreamed about owning this cottage for years. When I saw the foreclosure sign I nearly hyperventilated."

"Now the house is yours," AJ said.

Bailey grimaced. "Not quite mine yet."

He sighed. They'd been through this for the past two years. "You don't have to pay me back."

"I know I don't." Bailey looked at Emma. "But my big brother doesn't understand that I *want* to pay him back. A zero-interest loan is enough of a gift."

He shook his head. "My sister is stubborn like our father."

"She's not the only one," Emma muttered.

Bailey laughed. "You've got that right. It's a trait we've all inherited. Some more than others."

"What's that supposed to mean?" AJ asked.

Emma rose up on her tiptoes and kissed his cheek. "It means you're more like your father than you realize, but that's part of what makes you lovable."

Warmth flooded AJ, and likely spread a goofy grin across his face. Damned if this woman's opinion hadn't become his be-all and end-all. She thought he was lovable. He felt like Rudolph dancing his red-nosed reindeer self in circles after Clarice told him he was cute.

Good thing none of AJ's business rivals—or Libby—were around to see he'd gone totally, raving bonkers. Only his family was here, and he could avoid them another ten years or so. Easily. Especially without Emma pushing him to make nice.

* * *

Stupid. Stupid. Stupid. Emma couldn't believe she'd told AJ he was lovable. Thank goodness Bailey had been right there or he might have thought Emma meant it. She sort of did, but maybe he wouldn't figure that out. Or maybe he already had.

Darn the man. Emma balled her hands. Why did he have to be so nice and generous and well, lovable?

"Did you have enough to eat?" Lilah asked, sitting in a rocking Adirondack chair where she had a view of all the happenings in the backyard.

"Yes, the pulled pork sandwiches were great. The asparagus spears, too." But the delicious food couldn't compare to being included last night and tonight in the Cole family celebrations, a dream come true for an orphan like Emma.

"I hope you saved room for dessert. Bailey made shortcake from scratch. Marianne brought the strawberries and whipped cream."

"Sounds yummy." Emma patted her stomach. "But I'm going to need to go on a diet when I get home."

Lilah pshawed. "Nonsense. If anything you're a little thin. A couple extra pounds would be healthy. I'm sure AJ would agree, but let's leave him out of the discussion. It's a rare man who can say anything about a woman's weight without getting himself in trouble."

"Advice more men should follow." Emma picked up a garbage bag and tossed the paper plates from the picnic table inside. "I'm going to clean up so Bailey isn't left with a mess."

"Thank you, dear," Lilah said. "You fit right in, you know that?"

Emma wondered if her feet were still touching the grass. She didn't think so. "Thanks. That means a lot."

The words did. Emma wished she could stay in Haley's Bay forever, but nothing was real, not her being accepted into the Cole clan, not the kisses shared with AJ, not the feelings she was developing for her employer. Still, a bay-size part of her wished all of it were true. Especially dating AJ.

"Help Emma clean up." Lilah directed a pointed stare at Camden, Declan's twin sister.

The young woman wore her straight brown hair in a ponytail and no makeup on her pretty face. She dressed more like her brothers in oversize jeans and a long-sleeved T-shirt. But not even the baggy clothes could hide Camden's athletic physique and curves. Camden sighed. "I catch, gut, clean and fillet fish all day, Grandma. Isn't that enough? Let someone else help."

Lilah tsked. "You'll never get a husband thinking like that."

"I'm not in the market for a husband, Grandma. My life is fine the way it is."

"Well, I need more grandkids."

"Talk to Risa and Ellis. They've already got two and all the gear."

"Those children need cousins, not second cousins once removed, to play with. First cousins. Though if the rest of you keep taking your own sweet time, these kids will be old enough to babysit for you."

"Be glad you don't live in Haley's Bay," Camden said to Emma. "Or this grandkid talk is all you'd hear."

"Well, I'm not getting any younger," Lilah countered.

With a smile, Emma moved to a folding card table. The Coles weren't a perfect family, but they were real. In spite of their differences, they loved one another, even Mr. Cole and AJ, if either of them would put their stubbornness aside. The two men sat closer to each other. Progress? Emma hoped so. She picked up more plates and cups.

"I've been toying with a boating app," AJ announced.

"Lots of them on the market," Mr. Cole said.

Ellis nodded. "NOAA put out one with free nautical charts."

Her heart ached for AJ. He so wanted to impress his family, and when his efforts failed, he retreated, distancing himself or in this case, not saying a word. His actions had nothing to do with his family's rejection, but showed AJ's insecurities. The two of them might come from different worlds, but they shared something in common—loneliness. She hated how he'd separated himself from his family.

"What does your app do?" Declan asked.

Emma wanted to kiss the guy for asking. Not really, but AJ needed help from his family to find his way back home.

"Mine has charting and wind features as well as tides, and weather with animated radar," AJ explained. "The app is still in beta mode. It needs more testing."

"Come out with us tomorrow afternoon," Mr. Cole said. "We'll try it out."

Ellis nodded. "We can be your beta testers."

Please say yes. She clutched the garbage bag. They'd planned on going through Lilah's photo albums to scan and print pictures for the florist to use, but Emma could do that herself.

"Sure," AJ said finally. "That would be great."

Emma released the breath she hadn't realized she was holding. This was the first step for AJ to find his place here. She crossed her fingers, hoping he made the most of the opportunity.

AJ searched the backyard, but didn't see Emma. Bailey's cottage didn't offer many hiding spots. He doubted he'd find Emma under any beds. He smiled, eager to tell her about going out with his dad and brothers on the boat tomorrow after lunch. Knowing she'd be happy pleased AJ.

"Looking for Emma?" Declan asked.

"He's always looking for her," Grady teased. "I would be too if I were him."

AJ shook his head. "Have you seen her?"

"She's in the kitchen washing pots and pans," Ellis said. "My wife was delighted. She hates getting roped into KP duty. Says it ruins her manicure and dries out her skin."

"Not Emma." AJ glanced at the back door, wishing he could see her. "She's the definition of low maintenance."

"Ironic since you can afford to give her anything she wants," Ellis said.

"Sometimes that's how you know," AJ said. "Emma wants nothing from me."

Declan's eyes darkened. "She might be after your money. Being humble could be an act."

This was the perfect time to remind himself that Emma was acting the part of his girlfriend. This might be—was—temporary, but something had shifted between them today. AJ wasn't sure what. "She's not."

"And you know this how?" Grady asked. "When I was in Seattle with Grandma you didn't mention a girlfriend. Neither Bailey nor Camden knew and they talk to you almost as much as Grandma and Mom. Now you're bringing this woman home when you haven't been here in ten years."

"Emma is my assistant's best friend. Libby wouldn't steer me wrong." AJ looked at Declan. "Why the concern? You haven't cared what I've done for the past decade."

Declan rocked back on his heels. Ellis looked at the grass. Grady took a sip from his can of soda then glanced up. "Dad."

AJ looked at each of his brothers. "Dad?"

"Yes, me," his father said. "You boys get out of here. I need to talk to AJ alone."

Declan, Ellis and Grady scattered like ants on a picnic blanket, but not before Declan threw AJ a sympathetic glance.

His father sat in one of the camp chairs. "You went by the Candy Cave and saw Natalie."

AJ nodded.

"Did she tell you about her and Craig?"

Another nod. "Said they were separated, and he was seeing someone else. Wanted to know if I'd be interested in getting back together even though Emma was right there."

His dad whistled. "Not surprised by that. I'm assuming she didn't mention being the one who cheated?"

AJ's jaw dropped. "No."

"Saw her myself or I wouldn't have believed it. The guy dumped her as soon as Craig told her to get out. The Steeles are our biggest competitor, but I feel real bad for him. He's trying to get full custody of the two kids. Rough road ahead, but you sure dodged a bullet with that one."

"Yeah." AJ tried to wrap his mind around the fact Nat had wanted a second chance with him after cheating on her husband. But then again, she'd been wearing AJ's engagement ring when she went out with Craig. "I don't think I'll ever understand women."

"I gave up with your mother a couple decades ago," his father said. "Now Emma…"

His father's suspicious tone made AJ stiffen. "What about her?"

"Seems nice, but women have the ability to make us men stupid. Protect yourself, son. Have those fancy lawyers draft up a pre nup before your relationship goes any further."

He stared at his father as if seeing the man for the first time. "A pre nup?"

"Hell, yes," his dad said. "I didn't raise any fools though I had my doubts about Grady until recently. You've done well for yourself, son. Got a lot to lose. Don't get married until she signs a pre nup. Promise me."

His father had asked him for only three things: to stand up for his brothers and sister, to not go across the country for college and to take over the family business instead of moving to Seattle to work in technology. This was the fourth, and like the first, a no-brainer, especially since AJ never planned on marrying. Not Emma or any woman. "Sure. I promise I won't get married without a pre nup."

"Good. Very good." His dad stood. "Looking forward to seeing what that app can do tomorrow."

"Me, too," AJ admitted. "And, Dad, thanks for the advice."

His father nodded once. "Anytime, son. All you need to do is ask."

Maybe Emma was right. Maybe things could change.

Chapter Ten

Sitting on the swing the next morning, Emma kept her feet firmly planted against the porch to keep from moving. She held on to Blossom's leash, an old dog tether Lilah had in the garage. The cat had pawed at the window through the night, making sleep impossible for Emma. That and her sudden fascination with watching AJ sleep, but there was nothing to be done about that oddity. She hoped being out here at least appeased Blossom, who explored as far as she could, sniffing the air and rubbing against what she could. "Enjoy the outdoor time, but this isn't going to be a habit."

"I can't believe Blossom kept you up all night." AJ leaned against the porch rail, a cup of coffee in hand. He'd seemed more relaxed when they returned from Bailey's house last night. Maybe the thought of going fishing with his dad and brothers this afternoon had put him into a good mood. No matter what the reason, seeing him happy pleased Emma. "I didn't hear a thing."

She sipped from her cup of black tea, needing a jolt of caffeine to get going.

"That's because you were exhausted from staying up the night before. It was my turn." A blue sky with only a few puffs of white stretched to the horizon. Boats, big and small, headed out of the harbor for a day at sea. "Another gorgeous day in Haley's Bay."

"Summer is like this." He looked like the poster child for vacation apparel in his board shorts, a T-shirt and bare feet. "Some rain from storms off the Pacific, but days like today make up for the wet winters."

"Sounds like Portland weather. Late summer and early fall is my favorite."

"September was mine. Sunshine and school."

She drew back. "School?"

"New notebooks and pens and batteries for my drafting calculator."

"You're such a nerd."

"Computer geeks r us."

The angle of the sun's rays gave him a golden halo around his head. Talk about gorgeous. Emma sipped her tea. The warm liquid did nothing to cool her down.

"I couldn't wait for school to start." He bent over and gave Blossom a pat on the head. "Summer vacation was too long for me. Always too much fishing. You'd think my old man would've figured me out back then."

She'd never dreamed of any foster parent figuring her out. She hadn't wanted them to know her that well. Not all were bad, but those were the ones she remembered. "I liked being in school, too."

She received a hot breakfast and lunch at school. Sometimes an afternoon snack if whatever foster parents put her in extended care after school.

Blossom chirped, sounding more birdlike than feline.

She stared through the porch railing at two hummingbirds hovering around a feeder.

"You can look, Blossom, but you'll never get a chance to catch them."

The words didn't deter the cat. She crouched into a hunting position, her gaze never leaving the birds.

"She's ready to attack," AJ said, sounding amused.

Emma tightened her hold on the leash. "I wonder if her owner let her outside. She seems to like it."

"Sunshine, a breeze, birds." He moved to the swing, then sat next to Emma, his bare leg brushing hers. Sparks erupted at the point of contact. "What's not to like?"

She could say the same thing about him, except a little space would be nice so she wasn't the first spontaneous combustion casualty in Haley's Bay. She scooted to the far edge until her hip bumped the armrest. That still didn't give her more than a couple of inches between them.

AJ put his arm on the top of the swing. "Good idea bringing the cat out here. Though I'm enjoying it more than her. A nice place for my morning coffee."

She raised her mug. "And tea."

Blossom looked at Emma and AJ. The cat meowed once, jumped onto the small empty space between them then nudged each with her head.

Emma laughed. "Blossom is jealous."

"Cats don't get jealous. She wants more space."

"She wants you for herself."

AJ gave the cat a pat on the head. "Nice kitty."

The cat crawled onto his lap, circled once, then lay down. He rubbed the cat. Purring commenced, loud like a generator during a power outage. "Not jealous, sleepy."

"Sleepy, yes, but staking her claim." As if on cue, Blossom stretched. "She's made herself at home."

"A totally different cat from the one screeching on the flight here."

Emma could say the same thing about herself. She sipped her tea.

AJ set his cup on the railing next to the swing. "I asked my grandma if she wanted to adopt Blossom, but she thinks she's too old. Doesn't want Blossom to get attached and then grieve when she dies."

"Cats do grieve. Blossom has been through that with the passing of her last owner."

"Sounds more like an excuse. My grandmother likes to travel to see her kids, grandchildren and friends. A cat would mean added responsibility."

"I don't blame Lilah for wanting to have the freedom to do what she wants without having to worry about a pet. I can't have an animal due to my job. Not many clients want a live-in nanny who comes with their own dog or cat."

AJ's gaze narrowed. "I thought you'd want my grandmother to keep her."

"Only if Lilah wants Blossom," Emma explained. "The cat needs to be with someone who wants to adopt her, someone who will love her the way she deserves to be loved, not out of some sense of obligation. That's why I keep saying a forever home. Animals get attached. Change is hard on them."

"I see that, but having my grandmother keep Blossom would have been the easiest solution to my problem."

Emma liked AJ, but sometimes the guy didn't have a clue. "Blossom is not a problem."

"She is until I find her a place to live. Excuse me, a forever home," he corrected. "And no worries. We made a deal. I'm a man of my word, but I might not be able to find Blossom a forever home for her until I get back to Seattle."

"That's okay. I'll take her back to Portland with me.

I'm going to need approval for an out of state adoption anyway." Warmth balled in the center of her chest at the thought of the cat having a family of her own. "I appreciate you keeping your word."

"No need to sound grateful. This was something you wanted. I'm not doing it out of the goodness of my heart." He sounded like a CEO again. "I'm getting something out of this in return."

"I hope having a pretend girlfriend has been worth it."

"Best spur-of-the-moment decision I've ever made."

"You think?"

AJ nodded. "No drama. No need to buy presents. No talk about the future. Might have to try fake dating when I get home."

"Go for it." Her voice was flat, not encouraging, but the idea of AJ with another woman unsettled Emma. She stared into her tea. "Don't forget the big donation to the shelter. Pretending hasn't come without a price."

"A tax deductible donation is better than blowing money on some sparkly bauble I'll see only once or twice."

"You sound so jaded."

"No. Just the reality of my situation." He rubbed his chin. "Something my father reminded me of last night."

"Your dad talked to you? What did he say?"

AJ stared over the edge of his coffee mug. "He wants me to have my lawyers draw up a prenuptial agreement for you to sign."

"You're kidding."

"Nope." AJ half laughed. "He said I'd done well for myself and have a lot to lose."

"You do," she agreed. "Your dad is a smart man. Another way the two of you are alike."

He rubbed Blossom, who rolled over so AJ had better access to her tummy. Emma envied Blossom's proximity to AJ. All night she'd thought about curling around his warm body. Of course once they touched, those thoughts would have turned steamy, but from afar, all she wanted was the closeness.

"Knowing he's concerned must make you happy."

"I never thought he cared," AJ admitted. "I was surprised."

"Your father cares. Your grandmother and mom have told you that. But this is proof from your father. A man who doesn't care about his son would never bring up the need for a pre nup. He'd let you marry a gold digger and let her steal your fortune."

"Gold digger nanny?"

She shrugged. "It works for illustrative purposes."

Blossom's purring stopped. The cat slept soundly.

The silence was soothing, the lack of conversation comfortable.

Emma sipped her tea, staring at the bay. A bird swooped down to catch breakfast. She wondered if one of the boats she'd seen motoring out of the harbor earlier belonged to the Cole family, and if they were having any luck fishing.

"My family believes we're contemplating marriage," AJ said finally. "We're going to have to come up with a breakup scenario I can tell them after we leave."

Emma's heart panged. She didn't want to think about going home to her studio apartment alone. Not when she liked being surrounded by family and dreamed of being surrounded by AJ.

The corners of Emma's eyes stung. She blinked. Once, twice. Okay, that was better. "Don't get ahead of yourself. We have a couple of days left here. Someone might figure out we're not really dating."

"Won't happen. If my dad's talking about a pre nup, we've convinced them."

She giggled. "Hard to believe."

"I know."

"You can tell them we got tired of having a long-distance relationship but I didn't want to move to Seattle and you weren't moving to Portland."

"That'll work unless you move to Seattle."

"I don't know what I'm going to do. But your family would never know if I moved." The thought of never seeing Lilah or any of the Coles again made Emma's hand shake. A good thing the party was on Saturday. Getting attached to people she barely knew was beyond stupid. "But I must admit having a fake boyfriend has been more fun than I thought it would be. I'd forgotten how nice it is to hang out with someone. I'm going to have to get out more, make new friends when I'm back in Portland."

"Are you talking friends or men?"

"Both," she said. "Until now I haven't been…something. Willing? Ready? I don't know. But I want a real boyfriend. Our spending time together has been really nice."

She expected him to smile, but AJ didn't. "How do you usually meet men? Online?"

"No. I'm too…"

"Old-fashioned."

"Yes. I don't date much due to my work and being more of a homebody, but I'd rather meet someone in person or through friends or the rescue shelter." Talking about meeting other men felt weird, somehow wrong. But he'd asked so she wanted to answer. "Though I should figure out if I'm moving to Seattle first. Wouldn't want to meet the man of my dreams and then move away."

AJ stared at the cat. "Long-distance relationships are tough."

He would know after Natalie. "I've never been involved

in one. But don't you go out with women all over the world?"

"Yes, but I only date casually wherever I might be," he explained. "That's different than being in a committed relationship and not seeing each other every day."

"A fake relationship does have some perks, then."

"I like knowing the expectations ahead of time."

"Doesn't that put a damper on the overall romance with no spontaneity, no surprises, no future?"

His gaze locked on hers. "You've surprised me."

"You've surprised me, too." Self-preservation screamed to look away but she couldn't. Fake relationship or not, something connected them, something beyond Libby, the cat, his family and this trip to Haley's Bay.

Emma's pulse rate kicked up a notch. Her body's response to a glance, a touch, his kiss was one of those surprises. And her heart...

His arm slipped from the back of the swing to around her shoulder. "What if we expand our agreement?"

The bass drum *boom-boom-boom* of her heart turned into a snare roll. She opened her mouth to speak, but no words would come. Her tongue felt too big.

"I want to kiss you," AJ continued.

She looked around. "No one's here to see."

"Exactly."

The implication of his words bounced through her like a basketball. "We're just pretending."

"I know that's the deal. I also know I said I wouldn't touch you when we're alone. But I want to. Badly. That's why I'm asking. There's chemistry between us."

So he felt it, too. The realization didn't make her feel any better. "That doesn't mean we have to experiment. Some chemical reactions are highly combustible. Others don't react at all."

"Aren't you curious which we'll be?"

Emma was, and that scared her. She had a feeling there would be an explosion of epic proportions. AJ Cole wasn't like other men she'd known. Thoughts of him filled her mind and dreams. At times he left her feeling warm and fuzzy inside, but then he'd put her on edge and make her want to scream with frustration. His kisses frightened her most of all because in his arms she found a sense of belonging, a place that felt like home, somewhere she might want to stay. Forever.

But she knew better. There wasn't such a thing as forever. Nothing lasted. Not home. Not family. Not love.

Warning bells rang in her head. She wet her dry lips. "Curiosity can have serious consequences."

"One kiss without an audience, just you and me."

"And Blossom."

"She's asleep. No one will know. Not even the cat. It's only one kiss."

Emma hesitated, torn between following common sense and giving into desire. "One kiss saved Sleeping Beauty and Snow White, changed their entire lives."

"You into fairy tales?"

"Not at all, just…"

"Using them for illustrative purposes," he finished for her.

She nodded.

"We're past the first-kiss life-changing stage."

Emma wasn't so sure about that. AJ's first kiss had changed the way she thought about him, and each kiss since then. Since meeting him, a part of Emma wanted to believe happy endings were possible. Silly. She should know better.

"You're also awake, not under a spell," he added. "No magic in your nanny bag, remember?"

True, except being with AJ felt magical at times. A kiss, not a practice one or a pretend one but a for-real one, would let her know…

Emma wasn't sure what, but she might figure out something important. She wanted a kiss without anyone watching, without any reason or motivation for either of them, mainly him, to *perform*.

One kiss. What did she have to lose?

Taking the initiative, she leaned forward and kissed him. Man, he tasted good. Warm like sun shining down on them, with a hint of coffee—French roast. Yummy

He pressed his mouth against hers, deepening the kiss. His arm came around her shoulders. She pressed against him, arms circling him, wanting to get closer, wanting more.

One kiss. Oh, boy, this was so much more than a kiss. His lips breathed life into her heart. His touch made her feel desired.

Real, pretend, she couldn't tell the difference. The lines had completely blurred, and she didn't mind one bit. She could get used to this.

He moaned. Or maybe the sound came from her. Emma wasn't sure what was happening. She had never felt this away before and didn't want the feeling to stop.

His kiss ignited a fire low in her belly and heat spread through her. Hunger and need took over. She ran her fingers through his thick hair. Wanting to get to the place where it was only the two of them, and nothing else mattered.

"Mmmeorrrrrooooowwwrrrrreeee."

Emma jerked back. Her butt hit the porch with a loud thud. "I guess it doesn't get more real than this."

Blossom sat on AJ's lap as if nothing had happened. He looked stunned. "Let me help you."

Emma took the offered hand and stood. "Told you she was jealous."

"Her tail got caught between us. She didn't like that."

"For someone who claims not to like cats, you sure do stick up for her."

"Why do you assume the worst when you like her?"

"I..." Emma wasn't about to tell him he was wrong, except the sinking feeling in her stomach told her that he was right. "Maybe because I love cats and you hate them, but Blossom likes you better. Not quite fair, is it?"

"She likes you, too. You're the one she uses for a pillow at night."

"I'm softer."

"You also smell better, but stop trying to change the subject. Let's talk about the kiss." He stared at her, desire clouding his eyes, his breathing uneven. "I'd call it highly reactive."

An experiment she wanted to repeat. "I'd concur with that finding."

"We need more data points to explore this further."

Anticipation hummed through her. More kisses sounded great to her. But real kisses, any kisses, would complicate an already-convoluted situation. "We can't. I work for you. Exploring any more would be—"

"Inappropriate."

Dangerous, but she'd go with his reason. "Yes."

"But that kiss—"

"Was amazing." She wasn't going to deny the truth. "But we were never meant to be involved in a real relationship."

"Relationships are too complicated."

O-kay. She was missing something here. Not surprising given her lack of experience. Time to figure out what he meant by exploring this further. They might be talking about two different things. "What are you suggesting?"

"A fling."

"You want us to have a *fling?*" The word tasted like sand in her mouth.

"Yes. Stop working for me. Let's have fun together."

"Here? At your grandmother's house?"

"This is the perfect place given the time we have left here, and we have my grandmother's permission."

Emma's stomach churned. AJ didn't want her. He wanted to have sex with her. Why should she be surprised? He was not only attractive, but a billionaire who dated casually. To him, asking the pretend girlfriend sharing his bed to be his real-life lover during vacation would make total sense.

But to assume she'd be game… He didn't know her at all. The realization both hurt and angered her. Emma's blood pressure spiraled. "Thanks, I'm flattered, but no."

"No?"

His amazement in that one word made her bite back a smile. Having so much money must mean people never said no to AJ. Well, if that were the case, this would be good for him because he was going to hear the word again from her. "No."

He started to say something, then stopped himself. "Care to give me more than a two-letter answer?"

"Sure." Emma didn't want to aggravate him but she could give an hour-long speech as to why a fling would be a bad idea. "Playing make-believe is fine, but a fling is a good way to get hurt if real feelings become involved."

"I'm not looking for something serious."

Emma had never been seriously involved. But that was only because she hadn't met the right man. Okay, up until this point she hadn't wanted to meet the right guy, but after getting to know AJ, what she wanted was becoming clearer. "You're not looking for a committed relationship?"

"That's the last thing I want," AJ answered honestly. "I'm not sure I will ever have interest in that kind of relationship."

"You don't plan on getting married someday."

"No."

Relief pushed aside any disappointment. Her affection for AJ was growing and yes, he tempted her, but they wanted different things from relationships and life. Getting romantically involved with him would be a mistake. "Marriage is something I want. Having a fling would be a bad idea. I don't think I'd be able to keep my feelings casual, and even if I wasn't seriously involved I might miss meeting the man I'm supposed to marry. Trust me, my saying no is the best thing for both of us."

No. AJ stood at the harbor, waiting for the boat. Emma's rejection stung. She'd been firm, but nice. Still he rubbed his chin as if he'd been hit with a left jab.

No was a word AJ heard in business negotiations, from the board of directors, from this family. *No* was Natalie's answer when he begged her to wait until he returned to Haley's Bay after his freshman year before marrying Craig Steele. *No* was AJ's answer to women who wanted to get serious.

Emma's *no* meant she didn't want to get started with him. Her unwillingness to have a fling intrigued AJ. The way she kissed back told him she was interested.

So what was wrong with her? Didn't she know what he could offer her? Emma needed some fun in her life. She didn't have to take everything seriously, including romance. He wanted her to be happy. He wanted her to see that she was an amazing woman who deserved to have someone take care of her in return.

AJ could do all those things if she said yes. She wouldn't regret a thing. He had no doubt she would be thanking him when they were finished. All he needed to do was convince Emma to go from his bed buddy to vacation lover, but how?

Challenges revved his brain and kept his adrenaline high. This would be one of the best because of the reward he'd receive at the end. He had two days to change her mind.

AJ smiled, forming a plan of attack. Definitely achievable.

A horn blasted. Declan waved from the stern. Their father stood behind the wheel driving the boat to the dock. Memories of being picked up like this when AJ was a kid rushed back. Weekends and summer days spent out on the water. His dad had taught him and Ellis, then they taught Flynn, Declan, Camden and Grady. Bailey got too seasick to go out on the boat. Plus her wanting to wear skirts and dresses annoyed their father. Maybe AJ wasn't the only outsider.

"Climb aboard," his father yelled over the engine. "We're wasting time."

AJ jumped on board. He looked around. "Where are Ellis and Camden?"

"Out with tourists."

A few minutes later, his dad steered the boat through the mouth of the harbor. AJ enjoyed the ride. He hadn't been on the water like this in over ten years. He lifted his chin, letting the wind whip through his hair and over his skin. Spray shot up, wetting his sunglasses.

Declan adjusted his baseball cap. "Remember your way around?"

"Yeah." AJ wiped the saltwater from his sunglasses. "Don't forget who taught you everything you know."

"You mean Dad."

Declan's lopsided grin told AJ that his brother was kidding. "Hey, I might not have been the best fisherman in this family but I was one helluva teacher."

The engine cut off. His father climbed down from the helm.

"That's why you'd be great working with the tourists who don't know one end of a rod from the other and think every single fish they catch is a salmon." His dad stood next to him. "I sure as hell don't have the patience."

"Me, either," Declan admitted.

"So where's this app of yours?" Dad asked.

"On my phone." AJ pulled his smartphone out of his pocket. He wasn't exactly nervous, but he felt a strange sense of uncertainty, a way he hadn't felt since talking to his first venture capitalist. "I'll send you the app to load onto your phone tonight. I want your opinions, what works, what doesn't, any improvements you would make."

"Will it work on my tablet?" Dad asked.

Things really had changed around here if Jack Cole used a tablet. "Yes. It will."

Declan leaned against the bridge. "So show us what this thing can do."

With a deep breath, AJ handed his phone to his brother. "Here you go."

Chapter Eleven

That afternoon, Emma removed another photo from the scanner/printer she'd set up in the guest bedroom while AJ worked on his laptop. So far, Lilah was none the wiser to what was going on and thought Emma and AJ were making the most of their afternoon together.

She was. Just not in the way Lilah thought.

Emma enjoyed pouring through the Cole family photo albums filled with decades of snapshots, looking for ones to use for the birthday party decorations. The images and the time spent with AJ's family helped her clarify what she wanted in life. Something she never imagined happening during a temporary job as a personal assistant. A sigh welled inside Emma. If only she had someone to love her how she wanted to be loved... Someday she would.

She returned the photograph to the album and removed another picture. The candid with Lilah and one of her great grandchildren illustrated the passage of time. Emma remembered seeing a similar shot of Lilah holding the baby's father, Ellis.

Emma scanned the photograph. "So your dad and Declan liked the app?"

AJ glanced up from his computer. "They thought the app needed fine-tuning. My dad gave me a couple great ideas that I'm trying to incorporate. Declan, too. I can't wait for Ellis and Camden to try it tomorrow."

The excitement in AJ's eyes matched the smile on his face. Today had been a good day for him. Talking about his dad didn't seem to change AJ's mood, either. Emma couldn't be more pleased. He'd come so far in such a short time. She wiggled her toes. "I'm so happy things went well out there."

"Yeah, me, too. It went way better than I expected." He shook his head. "Except my dad still wants me back in Haley's Bay permanently."

"Of course he does. You're the oldest. His plans and dreams for you are still alive in his head and heart."

AJ nodded, and for the first time, didn't look upset over his father's expectations. Definite progress. "My dad asked if I'd go fishing in the morning. Said we'd dock by noon so there'd be plenty of time to get ready for the party."

"Better not stay up too late tonight. Sounds like it'll be an early morning."

"No."

"What do you mean *no?*"

"I told my dad I was on vacation and wanted to spend the day with my girlfriend preparing for Grandma's party."

Emma placed her hands on her hips, though sitting downplayed her annoyance. "Haven't you learned anything?"

AJ grinned wryly. "Is this when you take away my electronics before going all Supernanny and Nanny McPhee on me?"

"How could you say no to your father?"

"I never liked fishing much."

"That's not the point. Spending time with your family is.

"I can show up if I want, but I'd rather help you."

"I've got everything under control."

"You could use an extra hand. I've got two."

"If you change your mind—"

"I'm too stubborn for that to happen."

"Guess I deserve that." Emma pulled the sheet from the printer and added the picture to the manila folder containing all the printouts. "This is the last one."

AJ placed his laptop on the bed, then picked up the folder. He thumbed through the pictures she'd spent the day gathering and printing. "These are great. Grandma is going to cry when she sees these."

The photographs covered almost all of the past eighty years of Lilah's life. Emma had taken the most recent shots last night at Bailey's house. "Happy tears I hope."

"Tears of joy." He hugged Emma. "Thank you. These pictures are going to make her birthday party more special."

"You're welcome." She loved being in his arms, but was careful not to look at his face, especially not his lips. She didn't want him to think she'd changed her mind about wanting a fling. She hadn't, even if she couldn't stop thinking about him that way. "I enjoyed seeing the Cole family over the years. Grady was a cute kid."

AJ drew back. "Grady?"

"You were cute yourself." She stepped out of his embrace. "Can you please take the folder and flash drive to Charlie? He's waiting to drive these to the florist. She's working on the decorations tonight so they'll be ready tomorrow."

"Sure, but what about the photo albums?"

"Your grandmother's at the beauty salon with Bailey, Risa and Madison. Lilah will never know I borrowed them if I can get them back in the study before she returns."

"I'll run the stuff out to Charlie, then help you. We'll be done in no time." AJ slipped on his shoes. "Maybe we can take a walk before meeting my family at the pizza parlor."

"Sounds good." Lilah organized the albums by year, the way she'd found them. "We make a good team."

He stopped by the door. "We would make a better one if you'd say yes."

"Yes?" she asked, though she knew what he meant.

"To some horizontal experimentation with skin-to-skin contact. Should I go on?"

"Please don't."

"It's for your own good."

"Oh, really?"

"Yes. You work too hard. It's time to up the play factor in your life."

"That's what you're going with?"

"Damn straight." Laughter gleamed in his eyes. "Come on, doesn't some hot sex with a billionaire sound like fun?"

His flirty tone made her laugh. She had to give him points for not giving up. She appreciated how he wasn't pushing her, but keeping things light and playful between them. "My job is to look out for you. I like working for you, I don't want to quit, and don't you dare fire me. We work well as a team without the hot sex, in case you haven't noticed. That's why the answer was no, is still no and will always be no."

He feigned being shot in the chest. "Rejected once again."

"Stop asking and I'll stop shooting you down."

"Where's the fun in that?"

"I had a feeling that's what you would say."

"Of course you did," he teased. "Next time I need a pre-tend girlfriend I'll make sure she's not so old-fashioned."

"I'm sure there are millions of women who would be more accommodating than me when it comes to having a fling with a handsome billionaire."

"So you think I'm handsome?"

Darn, she hadn't meant for that to slip out. Too bad he didn't want to date, instead of having a fling, but Emma wouldn't go out with him, either. She liked him too much already. Opening her heart when she would be saying goodbye to AJ on Sunday would not be smart. "What can I say? You are easy on the eyes."

"Hold that thought. I'll be right back after I give these to Charlie." AJ left the room with the file in hand.

Emma carried the photo albums to the study and placed them back in the bookcase. This idea of hers had worked out well. She had another, too. She would load every picture she'd scanned today for the party decorations and slide show onto a digital frame for AJ to give to his grandmother as a birthday present. Emma would give AJ a copy of the JPEG files to store in case anything ever happened to the frame or the house. Having a backup was important. She wished her parents had put photo negatives into a safe deposit box somewhere.

The song from Disney's *Beauty and the Beast* sounded on Emma's cell phone. The ringtone was from the Lundberg twins' favorite movie. Her breath caught in her throat. Every nerve ending stood at attention as if a five-star general was walking past and needed to be saluted. Trey.

Why would Abbie and Annie's dad be calling? Emma hadn't talked to him in three months, not since she'd quit and moved out. She didn't want to look back. Looking forward to being home alone didn't hold much appeal, either. She wanted to make the most of the present here in Haley's Bay. She had only two more days.

The song continued to play. She slowly pulled out the phone from her back pocket. If she took her time, maybe Trey would hang up. He had no reason to be calling her... unless something was wrong with Abbie or Annie.

Adrenaline shot through Emma. She grabbed her phone, then hit Answer. "Hello?"

"It's Trey." His voice sounded rough, on edge, the way he'd sounded after a solo visit to his late wife's grave. After that, Emma had made sure she and the girls accompanied him. "Abbie was hit by a car."

Not sweet Abbie with her pigtails and toothless grin. Emma tightened her grip on her phone. "How badly is she hurt?"

"She had surgery yesterday. They moved her from ICU today. She's listed in serious condition."

Emma collapsed against the nearest wall in the study, sinking to the hardwood floor. An elephant rested on her chest. The weight pressed down on her breastbone, as if it were real, not imaginary. She wasn't sure what hurt more, breathing or her heart. But nothing she felt compared to Abbie's injuries and Trey's worry. "Oh, no. I'm so sorry. Does the upgrade mean she's stable?"

Let her be okay, Emma prayed.

"Yes, she's better," Trey said. "But seeing her unconscious yesterday... I'm sorry for not calling earlier, but Abbie was in ICU. Only immediate family is allowed."

Emma wasn't family. She was the former nanny. Of course she wouldn't be allowed in. "I understand. How's Annie doing?"

"Scared."

"That's understandable." Emma shivered, a chill over-coming her. "I'm sure you're all worried right now."

Arms encircled her, drew her close into a cocoon of welcoming, comforting warmth. AJ. She didn't know where he'd come from, but she was thankful he was here.

She leaned against him, wanting to soak up his strength. He might be her pretend boyfriend and wannabe lover, but she considered him a friend. And she needed one desper-ately at the moment. Emma had gone through so much alone. She didn't want to do that right now. Or ever again. "Where are you?"

"The children's hospital."

"I've been to their ER. Stitches for little Max. An ear infection for Samuel. An MRI for Brooklyn. They're the best when it comes to kids."

"That's what I've been told." Trey's voice cracked. "Keely is here. She's helping me with Annie."

Keely was the new nanny Emma had found. "That's great."

"Yeah, but ever since Abbie woke up from the surgery she's been asking for you. Annie, too. The girls wanted me to call and see if you could come by today."

"Of course, I'd be happy to come to the hospital. I prom-ised the girls I'd be there if they needed me." If the girls needed Emma, she had to go. She wanted to see Abbie and reassure Annie. Emma calculated the drive time back to Portland. Then realized she didn't have her car and also was obligated to AJ. She glanced at him. "At least I'll try to get there. I'm not in Portland."

"Go," AJ whispered. "It's not a problem."

Affection for the man next to her made her wish things could be different between them. She mouthed a thank-you, then returned to her phone conversation. "I'm in

Washington, across the river from Astoria, so it'll take me a little time to figure out a way there."

"As long as you'll come," Trey said. "It'll mean so much to the girls. And to me. The thought of losing Abbie…"

The pain in his voice stabbed her heart. A lump clogged her throat. She knew loss, that kind of paralyzing hurt and grief. Emma laced her fingers with AJ's, thankful he was here with her. She cleared her throat. "You're not going to lose Abbie. You said she's better. Stable. The girls need you to be strong, Trey."

"I know, but being here reminds me of Elizabeth."

Trey's wife, Elizabeth, had died of ovarian cancer. She'd been a stay-at-home mom who doted on her girls and her husband. Trey had never done more than give the twins an occasional bath, grill meat or wash a load of laundry until his wife had gotten sick. But Emma couldn't be Trey's support system again. That was likely the reason he'd fallen for her. "Focus on the girls. That's what Elizabeth would want you to do."

"I'm trying." He sounded so lost, like a rudderless boat adrift on the bay and heading toward the open water. "I don't know what I would do without Keely."

"I'm glad she's there to help you."

AJ squeezed Emma's hand, sending tingles shooting up her arm. She relished the feeling for a nanosecond, then refocused on the phone call. She liked Trey, appreciated what a good single father he was to his girls and how generous he'd been as an employer. He was handsome, but he'd never sent her blood boiling through her veins or made her want to give up her last breath for one more kiss like AJ.

But she realized with a start, the situation with the two men was similar. Both claimed they wanted her, but Trey wanted a fill-in wife and mother and AJ wanted a pretend girlfriend and vacation fling. Neither wanted her.

Not the way she wanted to be wanted. One man wanted her to complete his family. The other wanted her to be a willing casual sex partner. She didn't want to be either. She deserved…more. But until this moment hadn't known that. "Tell the girls I'll be there as soon as I can."

After a quick goodbye, she disconnected from the call.

"What's going on?" AJ asked, still holding on to her.

"One of the twins I used to nanny for was hit by a car. That was her father. She's in the hospital, doing better, but I promised the girls if they ever needed me I'd be there. I need to go. I'm sorry."

"Don't apologize. The jet will be the fastest way to Portland."

The room spun even though she was sitting. Emma leaned forward to keep from getting dizzy. "Th-thanks. That would be the quickest."

AJ used his finger to raise her chin. "You're pale and look scared to death."

She took a steadying breath. "I need to get to Portland. I'll be fine."

He didn't look convinced.

"Really." She tried to sound strong and in control. "I can fly for Abbie."

AJ's mouth twisted. "I doubt you've overcome your fear of flying since we arrived."

"I just don't like takeoffs," Emma clarified.

"Why not?"

The girls needed her. She scooted away from him. "There isn't time."

He pulled out his phone and sent a text. "There is time. The flight crew needs to be notified, a flight plan filed and the jet prepared for departure."

She'd forgotten flying had rules and regulations unlike driving a car. She wrung her hands.

"So why don't you like takeoffs?" he asked.

How hard could telling AJ be? They'd shared so much these past few days, moments beyond hot kisses and meaningful glances. She enjoyed being with him. Except her tight muscles and roiling stomach didn't seem to realize that.

"It's…" Her lips clamped together, as if tightened with a vise. She couldn't talk, not even if she wanted to tell him what had happened.

"Please, Emma." The concern in AJ's voice tugged at her heart. "Tell me."

She hadn't talked about what happened to her family since she'd stopped going to appointments with counselors and doctors. None of them understood what she'd experienced. No amount of talking or medicine would change the past. Her family and home were gone. Forever.

"Let me help you," he said.

AJ had protected Libby during the conference call on the jet. He'd made a large donation to the rescue shelter at Emma's request. His love for his grandmother and his family was clear, even if he wouldn't admit it.

Forget his Attila nickname. He wasn't a ruthless billionaire. The AJ she'd gotten to know was a thoughtful, generous, caring man. He wouldn't be able to help her beyond the use of his jet, but telling him why takeoffs affected her so badly was the least she could do to thank him for his getting her to Portland quickly.

"Libby told you I was in the foster system when I came to live with her and her parents, right?"

He nodded. "But she never told me what happened to get you there."

Emma inhaled deeply and blew the air out from her mouth. She did so again, mustering her courage and her strength. She could do this. With AJ at her side, she could do anything.

But she stared at the double-knotted laces on her tennis shoes, not wanting to see the familiar pity when people discovered she had no family. "When I was ten, my house caught fire. My bedroom was on the second floor. I remember being woken up by my brother, Michael. He was fourteen. I smelled smoke. Lots and lots of smoke. I could hardly see."

Emma rubbed her nose as if she could smell the scent now. "Mikey was a wrestler. Not that tall, but built solid and strong. He dragged me out of bed, pushed out the screen from the window, lifted me up to the sill and told me to jump."

"From the second story?" AJ asked.

"Mikey said there was no other way out of the house." Her hands trembled. She'd been terrified, clutching on to her brother's T-shirt with two hands, waiting for their father to come bursting into the room and save them. But he never came. It had been just her and Mikey. "I clung to my brother. Cried. He said he'd be right behind me. But I couldn't jump. Then he…he threw me out the window."

AJ sucked in a breath, gathered her closer. "Oh, Em…"

"As I fell, I heard screams. Awful, horrible screams." I wasn't sure if it was me or Mikey or my parents." She fought the urge to cover her ears. She knew the sound was in her memory and not real. "A loud boom sounded. An explosion. I expected Mikey to come to me, but he wasn't in the front yard. He wasn't anywhere. I looked back at the house to see it had collapsed. My brother, my mom and my dad were trapped inside. I never saw them again."

AJ held her, rubbed her arms, kissed her hair. "I'm so sorry."

"Me, too." She closed her eyes, thinking about her family, then opened them. "I don't remember what happened after that. I woke up in a hospital, but I've never forgotten that falling sensation. That's why I don't like to fly or go high on swings or ride roller coasters. I freak out and get sick."

"Understandable."

"After I recovered, I was put into the foster care system because there were no relatives to take custody of me. My parents had never written a will and appointed a guardian. I bounced around with different families for five years until Libby's parents became my foster parents the summer before my sophomore year of high school."

He caressed her cheek. "I noticed your smoke detector on the dresser, but had no idea."

The tenderness in his gaze made breathing difficult. "It's not typical dinner conversation. I've never told Libby everything. No one knows but you."

He brushed his lips across Emma's forehead. The gentle gesture warmed her cold insides. "Thank you for telling me. You've overcome a lot. You impress the hell out of me."

Emotion clogged her throat. She swallowed.

His gaze on hers, he looked like he wanted to kiss her. Her heart skipped a beat, maybe two. She could use a kiss. Desperately. Emma moistened her lips. Waited. Hoped.

AJ lowered his arm from around her. "Grab your purse and whatever else you need."

No kiss. Disappointment ricocheted through her. He hadn't wanted to kiss her, even though she'd wanted… No. She didn't want anything from him. Well, beyond a fast way to Portland.

He raised his cell phone. "With the birthday party tomorrow, I'm calling in the reserves to help."

"The reserves?"

"My brothers and sisters."

"But the party is my job."

"We're a team, remember? And in case you forgot, as I had until you reminded me, I'm part of a very large extended family. And so are you. It'll be fine."

Emma hoped so because all she wanted besides seeing the twins was to be a part of AJ's family. She tucked her hair behind her ears. "Thank you."

The limousine sped through town, a hair above the speed limit, but not enough to warrant a ticket from the officer on patrol, Grady, who waved as they passed. AJ had no doubt Charlie would get them to the airport in safe but record time.

In the back of the limo, AJ kept his arm around Emma. Her muscles remained tense beneath his palm. The tight lines on her face hadn't relaxed. She worried him. Hell, everything about this situation did from the injured child to Emma's tragic past. He patted her shoulder. "We'll be there soon."

"I'm sorry to leave you. I don't know if I'll be back tonight, but I'll try to return before lunch tomorrow."

Did she really think he would let her go alone? The thought boggled his mind. "I'm going with you."

Her lips parted. "But the party—"

"Is under control. Thanks to you."

Questions filled her gaze. Ones he wasn't sure he could answer if she asked. But the more he learned about her, the more he admired her. The more he wanted… "I want to help you."

And he would. Any way he could.

Her lips curved upward into a soft smile. "This is your vacation. Your first time home in ten years."

Her giving heart meant she thought of others before

herself. Whether that was the children she cared for or a person like him she'd met only a couple days ago. But someone needed to put Emma's needs first for once. He could do that. "My family understands."

"They think I'm your girlfriend."

"You are."

"Not really. Once we leave Haley's Bay…"

He brushed his lips across hers, fighting the urge to kiss her more deeply.

But she didn't need that now. "Don't think about that now. Lean on me. I'm right here. You're not going anywhere without me."

She rested her head against him.

The limousine turned into the airport and parked. Charlie hopped out of the car, then opened the passenger door. AJ followed Emma out of the car. Lights illuminated the tarmac outside the hangar.

She looked around, her eyes panicked. "Where's the jet?"

"No jet." He pointed to the waiting helicopter. "We're taking that instead."

"A helicopter?"

"It's not the same as flying in a plane. The momentum is different on take-off, more lift than propulsion. Might be easier for you. More distractions."

"This has gotta be costing you a lot of—"

"I've been thinking about getting a helicopter for a while."

"You bought this helicopter today?"

He nodded once.

Her eyes gleamed with gratitude. "Thanks."

"Just trying to help."

He'd spend as much money as it took to keep her from relieving a nightmare. "Let's go. The pilot is waiting."

She took a step toward the helicopter then stopped. Her body stiffened. "What if I get sick?"

"The pilot knows about your takeoff issues. He said we're good no matter what happens."

The look in her eyes made AJ feel like a superhero. "You think of everything."

"Not always." Except with Emma, AJ didn't want to forget anything. He wanted to do things for her himself, be in charge of all the details. "But this was easy."

He hoped the flight would be as easy for her. Buckled inside the helicopter with headphones on, AJ held Emma's hand. The rotor spun. Blood drained from her face, leaving her skin ashen. Her free hand balled into a fist, knuckles white.

He understood Emma's fear.

But if she didn't relax she would make herself sick again.

Emma needed a distraction. He knew what might work. All he needed to do was wait for the right moment.

The pilot made his final checks. Almost time for liftoff. This was it. AJ lowered his mouth to Emma's. So what if no one was around who needed to see them acting like boyfriend and girlfriend?

His lips pressed against hers.

So soft. And all his.

Yeah, kissing was the perfect distraction.

He wouldn't mind being distracted like this for the rest of today. Tomorrow. Every day.

Self-preservation screamed to stop kissing her. But he couldn't.

For Emma's sake.

Liar. He wanted to kiss her. For him.

He paused. They were airborne. "Good?"

She looked around. A grin spread across her face. "Really good."

"Let's not slack off now. There could be turbulence or a cloud…" AJ brushed against her mouth and nipped her lips open.

He might not get her into bed, but that didn't matter. Having sex with Emma wasn't the reason that he helped her get to the hospital. He was her friend. No ulterior motives involved.

What was happening to him? Emma had gotten under his skin. Even that damn cat was growing on him. Letting them go was going to be harsh, and unwelcome.

The realization made him deepen the kiss. He would give all he could and take what he could get. For now.

At the hospital, Emma skirted past AJ, who held open the door to Abbie's room. A cartoon played on the television, one of the girls' favorites. Trey stood next to the bed. Keely, the new nanny, sat on a recliner with Annie on her lap. Abbie looked so tiny in the hospital bed, tubes and wires connected to her bruised and broken body. Bandages covered her face. Gauze wrapped around her head. A cast was on her left arm.

Emma's heart tightened. Goose bumps covered her cold skin. She fought the urge to rub her hands over her arms and forced a smile instead. "Hello, everyone."

Annie jumped up from the chair, ran and threw herself against Emma. "You're here. I knew you would come. Abbie, I told you she would come."

Emma hugged the little girl. Sticky fingers touched her skin. "It's awesome to see you, Annie. You've gotten taller."

"I've missed you so much. Abbie has, too."

"Well, I'm here now."

"Yay." Annie wouldn't let her go. "Just like you promised."

"It's important to keep your word."

"I remember."

Emma let go of Annie, then kissed the girl's forehead. "Of course you do. You're a very smart girl."

Annie led Emma by the hand across the room to the hospital bed. "Abbie's going to be fine. Right, Daddy?"

"That's right, pumpkin."

Trey looked as if he'd aged ten years since Emma had seen him last. His usually coiffed hair was disheveled, as if the strands hadn't seen a comb in days. Whiskers covered his normally clean-shaven face. But the worry clouding his gaze and the deep lines at the corners and around his mouth surprised her the most. He looked wary, exhausted, ten years older.

"Hey, sweet princess." Emma touched the injured girl's left pinkie, one of the few places that didn't have any bruises or cuts. "It's so good to see you."

Abbie's dry lips formed an *O,* then curved upward. "Emma."

A lump burned in her throat. "I'm here, baby."

"Annie said you'd come." Abbie's voice sounded hoarse and weak. "All I had to do was ask."

Emma's chest tightened. She picked up the water cup and stuck the straw in Abbie's mouth. The girl sipped. "I'm sorry you're hurting."

The straw fell from her lips. "Better me than Annie."

Tears stung Emma's eyes. "You're such a good sister."

"Like you taught me to be." Abbie moved her hand to hold Emma's.

Trey gasped. "She moved her hand."

Keely touched his arm, a gesture of comfort and sympathy. He wrapped his arm around her and pulled her close so her head rested against his shoulder. The two looked more like a couple than an employer and employee, but their relationship was none of Emma's business. She was here for the girls, nothing else.

"I need to get the doctor," Trey said, then walked out of the room.

Emma focused on Abbie. "Are you as tall as Annie now?"

"Taller."

AJ stood next to the bed. "So this is Abbie."

Abbie's eyes widened. Her dry lips parted. "It's Prince Eric from *The Little Mermaid*."

"I'm AJ," he said. "Emma's friend."

"It's Prince Eric," Abbie said again.

Annie studied AJ with a discriminating eye. "My sister's right. You look like Prince Eric."

From the expression on AJ's face, he didn't have a clue who they meant. Emma took the opportunity to study him. "You know…the girls are right. Well, if you transformed yourself into a cartoon character."

"Who is Prince Eric?" AJ asked, sounding confused.

Annie giggled. "Emma's favorite prince."

"My favorite from the Disney princess movies," Emma clarified.

Trey returned. "The doctor will be right here. This is the most alert Abbie's been. Thank you so much for coming, Emma. You brought a friend?"

"Oh, my goodness." Emma let go of Annie. "Where are my manners? I totally forgot to introduce all of you."

"You were concerned about the girls," AJ said.

Trey extended his arm. "Trey Lundberg."

The two men shook hands. "AJ Cole."

"That name sounds familiar." Trey's mouth quirked. "The tech mogul. The one your friend works for."

"Emma works for me, too," AJ said.

"I'm filling in for Libby." Emma didn't want to get into too many details. This wasn't the time with Annie plastered against her side and Abbie holding her hand.

"You've met Abbie. This pretty princess is Annie." Emma motioned to the nanny. "That's Keely."

"Nice to meet you, AJ." Keely stared at Emma. "Your coming so quickly means the world to the girls and us."

Us. Definitely a couple, especially if the sparkling diamond engagement ring on Keely's hand was from Trey. Emma had to admit the two looked good together.

Trey cleared his throat. "The doctor will be here shortly. Could you take Annie to the cafeteria for a few minutes?"

"Yes," Emma said. "We'll have a snack."

"Ice cream." Annie shimmied her shoulders. "I want ice cream. Emma loves ice cream."

"I didn't know that," AJ said.

Annie nodded. "Rocky road is Em's favorite."

Emma pushed a strand of hair off Abbie's face. "It's true. But do you know my second-favorite flavor?"

"Butter pecan," Trey answered, to her surprise.

"How did you know that?" she asked.

"There was always a pint of that and one of rocky road in the freezer. The girls only eat chocolate or cookie dough."

Annie tugged on Emma's arm. "Can we get ice cream now? Please?"

Emma leaned over the bed to whisper into Abbie's ear. "We'll be back in a few minutes. As soon as you feel better, I'll take you for ice cream. Okay?"

Abbie gave a half nod.

Emma held Annie's hand as they exited the room. The little girl looked up at AJ. "What's your favorite ice cream, Mr. Prince Eric?"

"Rocky road," he said.

"Just like Emma."

His gaze met hers, a tender glance full of affection. "We have lots in common."

Emma's pulse quickened. "Do you like butter pecan, too?"

"No, but I don't mind black walnut."

Annie beamed. "You both like nuts. I like peanuts."

"What about hot fudge?" AJ asked.

The girl nodded, her ponytails bouncing furiously.

"Emma likes chocolate, too." AJ winked. "I saw her having seconds of my grandmother's brownies."

"I only had two."

He laughed. "You could have had more."

Emma wished she could have him.

Wait. What was she thinking? She wasn't. That was the problem. Her worry about Abbie was no excuse. Kissing most of the helicopter ride had addled Emma's brains. She needed to be more careful around AJ. Much more careful.

"I'm hungry," Annie said.

Emma realized she'd mentally drifted away for a moment. Something she had a habit of doing when AJ was around. She looked at the little girl and fought the urge to sniff the strawberry shampoo scent in Annie's hair. But Emma couldn't get too close. She was no longer their nanny. "Let's find you some ice cream."

Chapter Twelve

In the hospital gift shop, AJ bought stuffed animals for both girls and a bouquet of flowers with Get Well balloons for Abbie. He returned to the room to find Trey and Emma gone. AJ gave the presents to the girls, earning him smiles, thank-yous and a hug from a bear.

Annie curtsied, cuddling her stuffed bear like a baby. "Thank you, Mr. Prince Eric."

"You're welcome." He bowed. "Fine princess."

Abbie's frog sat next to her on the pillow while a nurse checked her vitals. The girl stared at the flowers with a smile on her bruised face. AJ would make sure fresh flowers and balloons were delivered every day during Abbie's recovery.

"You didn't finish telling me about the ice cream," Keely said to Annie.

"We had two scoops of ice cream." The girl bounced from foot to foot, making AJ wonder if she needed to use the bathroom, but Keely didn't seem alarmed. "Two big scoops."

"Did you eat all the ice cream?" Keely asked.

"Every last bit. I had chocolate with whipped cream and a cherry. Emma and AJ both had rocky road. That's their favorite. But they didn't want whipped cream or a cherry. I don't know why they wouldn't want a cherry. That's the best part."

Keely toyed with Annie's pigtail. "Did the ice cream taste good?"

"Oh, yes. The best."

"Sounds like special ice cream."

"It was." Annie lowered her voice. "Especially since Mr. Prince Eric bought me a soda to drink."

"Wow." Keely touched the little girl's shoulder, reminding him of Risa interacting with her two kids. Emma had been attentive, but not as warm and fuzzy with Annie downstairs in the cafeteria. "Ice cream with a soda would be the best."

"I know." Annie held up her bear. "And he also got me this."

Keely shook her head. "So cute."

"Abbie loves her frog already."

"Frogs are very special," Keely said. "Just like bears."

"Special like you and Emma." Annie hugged Keely. "Though you get to be my new mommy, not just my nanny."

AJ watched the two and realized there was a slight disconnect, a distance, in the way Emma interacted with the two girls. Oh, she cared about Abbie and Annie. Emma's coming to the hospital at a moment's notice was proof of that, but Keely acted more like a mom while Emma seemed—he searched for a word—*guarded*. No, perhaps *professional* was a better description, since Emma was nurturing and affectionate. But not even that adjective truly fit, because someone who was only doing their job wouldn't be here or trying to get him to reconcile with his family. Maybe he was off base. Except…

Looking back on his three days with Emma, he noticed a contradiction. She wanted to know personal details and stick her nose into his business, but she offered nothing of herself in return. Granted, he hadn't asked many questions, but when he did, she was good about changing the subject or turning the focus onto someone else, mainly him.

Today, he'd dragged the information about her family out of Emma. She'd likely relented because she needed to steel herself for the flight on his jet, not because she wanted him to know anything about her.

The realization bugged him. He'd seen her go out of her way to help others and not ask for anything in return. She had to have needs…dreams, especially growing up the way she had. He wanted to make her dreams come true.

The door opened, and Emma walked inside the room followed by Trey. The two talked quietly, as if sharing a private moment. Okay, not so private given they weren't alone, but who knew where they'd been a few minutes ago. They seemed comfortable around each other. AJ's stomach tightened.

Trey must like nannies if he was marrying Keely. Had he also dated Emma? Was that why she didn't want to have a fling? She'd had her heart broken or didn't want to be hit on by another boss? AJ didn't like either scenario. He balled his hands, wanting to punch something. Well, Trey.

Emma walked toward AJ while Trey headed straight to Keely and the girls. "We spoke to the doctor," Emma kept her voice low. "Abbie's doing better. She'll be hospitalized for a while during her recovery, so I can see her once I'm back in Portland. There's no reason we can't return to Haley's Bay right now."

"You don't want to stay longer?" AJ asked.

"No." She glanced at Trey, Keely and Annie standing next to Abbie's bed. Hurt flashed in Emma's eyes. "It's time for me, for us, to go. The birthday party's tomorrow."

Emma spoke with zero emotion, treating this hospital visit like a job or item on the to-do list she kept in her notebook. Something was off, but AJ didn't know what.

He pulled out his cell phone and typed a message. "I texted the pilot."

"Thank you."

She glanced at the foursome. The longing in her eyes about broke AJ's heart. He touched her arm, wishing he could kiss her and make everything better. "What's wrong?"

"I'm ready to get back to Haley's Bay. That's all."

Emma might believe that, but he didn't. Something was bothering her. He leaned closer, placing his mouth right next to her ear. "Is it Trey and Keely?"

"Heavens, no." Emma lowered her voice more. "Trey told me about their engagement. I'm thrilled for them and the girls. We never… He wanted to, but I didn't. Everything's worked out for the best."

Laughter sounded from the other side of the room. Emma sighed with a wistful expression, not a look of jealousy.

"Something's still bothering you," AJ said.

"It's…" Emma shot a sideward glance toward Abbie's bed. "I'm not bothered. I'm envious of Keely getting a family. That's all."

Emma might not buy into fairy tales, but she had a favorite prince and, according to Annie over ice cream, knew all the princess movie song lyrics by heart. The nanny—his nanny—was a romantic who'd lost her family and wanted another.

AJ nearly laughed, and not in a good way. He could

give Emma anything money could buy. Hell, he'd bought a helicopter and hired a pilot to bring her to Portland today, but he couldn't give her the family she wanted.

Still, he wanted to help her. Who was he kidding? AJ wanted to take Emma home. Not back to Haley's Bay. To his home in Seattle. Where he wanted her to stay. With him.

This was never going to work. AJ combed his fingers through his hair. She wanted a family. He didn't want a relationship. Unless they... Maybe they could compromise. Business deals and mergers had been mediated. He'd compromised with internal projects. External ones, too. For a chance with Emma, he was willing to try anything.

Fifteen minutes later, after hugs and kisses and good-byes had been exchanged in Abbie's room, Emma waited with AJ at the helicopter pad. She needed a nap, a good cry, a hug, a kiss and dinner. Not in that particular order. "I'm so glad Abbie's doing better."

"I hear the relief in your voice." AJ put his arm around her shoulder. "Just when I think you can't impress me anymore, Emma Markwell, you do. You're amazing."

"I don't know about that, but thanks. You're pretty amazing yourself." Somehow she managed to say the words without her voice croaking or cracking or squeaking. Maybe she could do without the nap. "Buying the girls presents was very sweet. The stuffed animals were adorable, and the bouquet was beautiful. Did you see how Abbie kept staring at the flowers?"

He nodded. "They seem like great kids."

"They are. A couple of my favorites."

"How long did you work for the Lundbergs?"

"Nine months." Thirteen days and four hours, but who was counting?

"Not that long."

Emma shrugged. "Some nannies stay in positions for years, until the kids no longer need them or the family can't afford them, but I've never worked for more than twelve months. Most of my assignments are shorter. That's my choice."

AJ straightened. "That's it."

"What's it?"

"I noticed a difference in how you and Keely interacted with the girls. I don't mean this in a negative way—it's something I noticed when you were in Haley's Bay, too."

"What are you talking about?"

"You hold a piece of yourself back."

"From you?"

"From everyone. The families you work for, the children you care for, the people you meet."

"That's not true. That's ridiculous." She stared down her nose at AJ, offended. "I put everything into being a nanny. I pour all of me into each child. Aren't I here now?"

"You are. That meant everything to the girls, but you keep walking away from families."

Her cheeks felt warm, her chest heavy. "I don't walk away. I tell them my availability from the beginning. It's their choice whether they want to hire me or to keep looking for someone longer term."

"Their choice? Before you said it was your choice," he repeated her words.

"No." She shook her head, more like a three-year-old. "Stop attacking me."

"I'm trying to help you the way you've helped me," AJ said. "Think about it. Think about all those kids you said you took to the ER. Think about Abbie and Annie."

"No. I…" Emma covered her face with her hands. Her limbs burned as if on fire. "Oh, no. You're right. That's exactly what I've been doing and I didn't even realize it. I gave my love for them a time limit. Those poor kids."

AJ cradled her in his arms. "It's okay."

"No, it's not." She rested her head against his shoulder, wanting to hide away from the world. Time for a career change. Something different. "I was supposed to be nurturing and caring and devoted—"

"You were all those things today with the girls. Annie said you were the best nanny ever, even better than Keely. I'm sure the kids never realized what was going on. You've been those things with my family and me in Haley's Bay, but for some reason you don't open yourself completely and let others in."

"I—I don't want to get too attached." So many things made sense now. She rubbed her face. "I think that's why I bolted when Trey said he wanted to date me. He gave me a reason to leave. I never stuck around long enough to see if things would be awkward or not. I just ran."

"That makes two of us. You ran from the families you worked for. I ran from my family and Haley's Bay."

"I'd laugh if it wasn't so sad." She shook her head. "We're a pair."

"A pretty good pair if you ask me. You helped me figure out things with my family. Now I've helped you."

"You did. But ouch, it kinda hurts."

"Should have warned you about that."

She kissed his cheek. "Thanks anyway."

"There's something else we need to work out."

"What's that?"

"Us."

Her shoulders sagged. She didn't want to rehash this morning's discussion again. "I'm not the fling type. Nothing else needs to be said."

"How about I'm sorry?" he asked. "I know a fling isn't for you."

"I've been worried I gave you the wrong impression by sharing your bed or kissing you back."

"You didn't. This is my fault completely."

His words brought a rush of relief. Maybe things could be different between them. She crossed her fingers. "An easy mistake to make when you haven't known someone long."

"It might not be long, but I know I want to spend more time with you."

Her heart stumbled. She was afraid to hope. Nothing had worked out before. Well, nothing except Libby and her parents. "We don't have much time left in Haley's Bay."

"True, but we have plenty of time after we leave."

"I'm confused."

"You're cute when you crinkle your face like that."

She touched the bridge of her nose. "It's just…we want such different things."

"You want marriage and a family. I don't want a relationship."

"Exactly." Hope deflated like a Mylar balloon with a pinhole. Slowly. She'd rather the whole thing just blow up. "It will never work."

"Not all relationships end in marriage," he explained.

"No, but that's always a possibility, right?"

"Maybe not."

"I'm more confused now."

"What if we got to know each other. Dated. Dinners, movies, art shows, a show on Broadway or beignets in New Orleans?"

"We live in different states."

"Dating would be easier if you moved to Seattle. That's where the first compromise comes in."

His tone bothered her. She narrowed her gaze. "You sound like you're negotiating a business deal."

"More like a relationship."

That got her attention. She couldn't believe he'd said the word. "You don't want one of those."

"If dating works out, and we decide to pursue something more, I would be willing to compromise."

"In what way?"

"I'd agree to a relationship with you if you forgot about having a family with me."

His words seem to be punctuated with a gong. The air felt heavy in her lungs. She struggled to breathe. "Are you serious?"

He nodded. "Move to Seattle. We'll get to know each other. Date for real. Then take it from there."

Unreal. Emma couldn't believe a man who made her realize something so crucial about herself could be so, so, so stupid and shortsighted and selfish. "Take it where? To a relationship with no chance of a future?"

"Marriage doesn't equal the future."

"No, but you're asking me to compromise on my dream so I can hang out, have you support me, fly around on your jet and sleep with you."

He flashed her a devilishly charming smile, one she wanted to wipe off with a tissue. "You have to admit it's a good compromise."

Not good. She rested her face in her hands. Not by a long shot. What if she fell in love with him and wanted more? He wouldn't give her more. He wouldn't ever give her his heart.

I like knowing the expectations ahead of time.

His words echoed in her mind. She wouldn't be surprised if AJ had this whole *relationship* thing planned out from beginning to end. Speaking of which… "How long do you see this lasting?"

"As long as we're having a good time."

That could mean four days or four years. This wasn't a compromise. This was a temporary arrangement for the benefit of one person—AJ Cole. She would wind up with nothing except a broken heart, a few memories, ticket stubs and shiny baubles he'd tell another woman he regretted buying. Her temper spiraled.

The helicopter approached.

"You are an amazing man, Atticus Jackson Cole. I thought you were my friend. I thought you'd figured me out even though I held back on you. But I was wrong on both counts. You are used to getting what you want. This time that happens to be me. But I'm not going to be flattered or compromised into something I don't want."

"Emma—"

"Let me finish." She didn't have much time with the helicopter landing. "Being with you in Haley's Bay has been wonderful. I'm not going to deny that. You've helped me learn so many things about myself, including what I want. I need to put myself out there if I'm going to fall in love, get married and have a family. I can't be afraid. I can't settle for less. I definitely can't compromise with some half-hearted, never-going-anywhere relationship designed to end when it's no longer fun."

AJ's jaw hung open. "You're as stubborn as my dad."

"As stubborn as you."

"I like you."

"I like you, too." She patted his hand. "This isn't a rejection. We both know what we want. They happen to be different things. That's okay."

"There's chemistry between us."

"Sparks ignite the flame, but someone needs to tend

the fire to keep it going." She squeezed his hand. "I need to find someone who will want to collect more wood and kindling and tend with me. Not use semantics to get out of doing the job or hire someone else to do it for him."

His lips thinned. "I thought you cared about me."

"I do." Shutting up was what she would normally do, but not any longer. She needed to open up. This was a good place to start. "I'm sure if I let myself I could fall in love with you quite easily."

He inhaled sharply.

"But I'm not a deal you can negotiate or company you can acquire with terms favorable only to you," she continued. "I'm not something that can be compromised. I agreed to be your pretend girlfriend and I will continue to do that. But do not touch me and you better not kiss me unless you want a black eye."

Six o'clock the next morning, AJ stood at the harbor waiting for his brothers and dad to show up at the boat. He hadn't planned on going fishing, but now that Emma had kicked him to the curb for the second time—hell, forever—he knew better than to hang around. She had the party under control. He was only in the way.

But he missed her already. Not because he felt a sense of loss that something he wanted wasn't around. He was missing the partnership. Half of being a team, of something... special. The thought of saying goodbye to Emma tomorrow was killing him. He couldn't let her walk away, but how could he stop her?

"Look what the cat dragged in." Ellis laughed. "Surprised to see you up this early."

"What the hell?" Declan slapped AJ on the back. "You look worse than some roadkill I've seen."

"Woman trouble, son?" his dad asked.

AJ nodded. He'd been running away like Emma, but he was ready to stop, change, set things right. Her words had been echoing through his head all night.

Until now I haven't been...something. Willing? Ready? I don't know. But now I want a real boyfriend.

Marriage is something I want, which is why having a fling is a bad idea. I can't keep my feelings casual.

She'd told him exactly what was going on, what she wanted, but he hadn't listened. He'd proposed the exact opposite to her twice. Idiot.

AJ was an idiot for trying to get Emma to have a fling she didn't want and a relationship with no future because he didn't want those things, either. He wanted the bigger dream. He just hadn't realized it yet. But now he did. Oh, man, did he.

He was head over heels for Emma Markwell. What he felt for her after four days was different than the aggrandized, childish love he'd felt for Nat and different from the lust he'd experienced for other women. Falling so hard so quickly was the last thing he expected to happen, but exactly what he needed. There had to be a way to make things right.

"I messed up with Emma." The anguish in his voice matched the pain in his heart. He hadn't planned on her touching that particular organ, but somehow she had and he couldn't imagine life without her.

"Come on," Declan said. "She's crazy about you. Buy her a dozen roses and a diamond and all will be forgiven."

"That won't work. Not with her," AJ explained. "I'm not sure what will. I only met her four days ago."

His father and brothers' jaws dropped in unison.

"Four days and I'm already in love with her," AJ continued. Emma had shown him how much was missing from his so-called perfect life. He'd been so focused on work and increasing his company's bottom line, he'd forgotten to live and to love. She and that cat of hers had been affectionate and devoted to him. He'd been happier in Haley's Bay, in the town he thought he hated, because of them. That had to be love, right? "Either that or I'm losing my mind."

"Sounds like love to me," his father said, resigned.

"But I screwed up and she wants nothing to do with me."

"Been there, done that, skipped buying the T-shirt." Ellis nodded. "Definitely love."

"I need to win her heart and get her back, but I don't know how." The words poured from AJ's lips. "I need your help."

His father put his arm around AJ's shoulder. "Let's get on the boat. Once we drop the lines, we'll formulate a plan. With all of us Coles working together, Emma doesn't stand a chance. She'll be yours before your grandmother blows out the candles on her birthday cake."

AJ sure hoped so. He would be happy if she agreed to give him another chance, but he liked his dad's outcome better.

The party was in full swing, and Lilah was the proverbial belle of the ball. Emma loved seeing the birthday girl, floating on air in a gorgeous lavender dress and a huge smile lighting up her face. Lilah danced from person to person soaking up the birthday wishes and love offered by family and friends. And she adored the pictures used in the party decorations. Lilah's happy tears had made up for Emma's sadness over leaving Haley's Bay tomorrow and having to say goodbye to the Cole family, including AJ.

"You've done well, girl." Mr. Cole stood next to Emma. "I don't think anyone will be able to outdo the soiree you put together. Thank you from my brothers and sisters and our kids and their kids."

"AJ's the host."

"I'm sure it wasn't my son or that capable city girl assistant of his who came up with the new theme at the last minute."

"Not last minute. Three days ago," Emma corrected. "As soon as I met your mother, I knew Lilah needed a unique and personalized theme. Something that was all her. Fortunately the vendors were willing to work with me at the last minute to make this an eightieth birthday party she'll never forget."

"Haley's Bay will never forget this. Great job." Mr. Cole headed to the bar.

Emma looked around at the family and friends enjoying themselves, especially Lilah. The nostalgic decorations, inspired by her photographs, brought laughter and tears. The food, based on recipes she'd cooked her family and neighbors over the years, started debates on who cooked the dishes better, Lilah or the caterer. The music, chosen from each decade of her life, kept people on the dance floor song after song.

Emma was both proud and miserable at the same time. At least AJ was enjoying himself.

He'd thanked Emma for her hard work, then walked away. Probably for the best. She'd shot him down, rejected him. Was it any wonder he'd run from her like he'd always run from his family and Haley's Bay before?

The two of them circulated separately the entire evening. He wore his host hat, visiting with guests and making sure Lilah was feted like a queen. Emma donned an imaginary event planner apron, overseeing the party schedule and keeping the DJ on track with announcements.

Being apart from AJ was good, she told herself. She

needed to get used to being apart from AJ after being with him almost nonstop since they'd arrived in Haley's Bay. He didn't seem to mind being away from her. Especially not now. He danced with Madison, who hung on his every word as well as his body. Emma tried not to care. Thinking about AJ hurt.

No worries. After tomorrow she would never see him again. The realization made her heart ache more.

"Wonderful job, Emma." AJ stood at her side. "If you decide you want a break from being a nanny, you should try event planning."

"Thanks." She had to force the word from her dry throat. "Lilah looks happy."

"Grandma is thrilled," he said. "She loved the digital frame with the pictures you uploaded. Thank you for coming up with the perfect birthday gift for her."

"You're welcome."

Talking to him hurt. Emma pressed her arms against her side. She didn't want to care about AJ. She wanted him to go back to the dance floor with Madison. Okay, not really. But chitchatting as if nothing had changed between them was hard. Especially since she was still supposed to be his girlfriend.

The DJ put on the song "What a Wonderful World."

"This was my mother's favorite song," she said without thinking. "She and my father danced to it at their wedding."

AJ extended his arm. "May I have this dance?"

She noticed his parents and siblings watching them. Madison, too. Emma couldn't say no if they wanted to keep up the charade. Only a couple more hours. She ignored the pang in her heart, took his hand and followed him to the dance floor.

He placed one hand on her waist as they took a traditional dance position. "I've had a change of heart."

"About?"

"Blossom."

Her gaze jerked up to meet his.

"I've found her the perfect forever home."

"Where?" she asked.

"With me."

Emma stumbled over her feet, but AJ kept her upright. "What are talking about? You don't like cats."

"I might not like cats, but I love Blossom. I spoke with the shelter earlier today. I'm adopting her."

Emma's heart tore a little more. A selfish reaction. She should be ashamed. Living with AJ meant Blossom would have the best of everything—food, toys, cat trees and veterinary care. "Diva Kitty hit the adoption jackpot."

"Glad you think so."

Emma nodded. But a part of her wished Blossom could stay with her. Being temporarily involved in a family as a nanny or part of an animal's life as a foster or shelter volunteer was no longer enough. She wanted a place to call home for longer than her typical three-month lease, furniture that didn't come with an apartment, a pet that she could provide a forever home to. How had her life become so...transitory? Was that her way of keeping her distance?

"I spoke to the shelter director this afternoon. Blossom's former owner built her an outdoor play area. He also took her to his office each day."

"Looks like you have a new carpool buddy."

"Yes, but I don't think Blossom's going to happy without you." AJ spun Emma around the dance floor. "Would you consider making our arrangement more permanent?"

She stopped dancing, unsure whether to be upset or happy he wanted to employ her after all they'd been through. "What do you want me to do? Be a cat nanny? Or do you want to continue the dating charade?"

"I don't want you to work for me. Though Emma Markwell, the billionaire's nanny, has a nice ring to it."

She gave him a look.

"I'll just come right out and say it." He cupped her cheek. "I love you, Emma."

Her heart slammed against her chest. Air rushed from her lungs. She held on to his hand, afraid if she let go her knees would turn to taffy again. "W-w-what?"

"I screwed up. But my family knocked some sense into me. Dad and Ellis told me they knew right away when they met their future wives, and I do, too. I can't let you go. Please give me another chance. And another chance after that when I screw up again. We Cole men can be dense, but I'm sure you'll straighten me out eventually. Please give me a lifetime of changes with you."

She struggled to breathe. "But that would mean—"

"A forever home for Blossom with me and you."

Emma sucked in air. Hyperventilating seemed inevitable.

"We haven't known each other long, but I hope you will someday feel the same way about me," he added.

"I…I…" Emma couldn't speak. She was stunned. Thrilled. Frightened to death. Her first instinct was to run out of the big white tent on the bluff and not stop until she reached Portland. Because what she wanted most in life were the things she feared losing again—a home, her things, a family, her pets. Things she could have with AJ.

Did she dare take that chance? Make the leap?

Self-preservation screeched no. She'd been listening to that voice since she was ten years old, and knew the reasons well, but seeing the Cole family, especially Lilah with her children, grandchildren and great-grandchildren, helped Emma to realize that the risk of loving and losing was natural. Living a solitary life with zero attachments and few possessions wasn't. She couldn't imagine walking away from AJ again.

He waited for her answer, his gaze never wavering from hers.

"You're serious," she said finally.

"Very."

She took a breath.

"I'm going to need a few chances myself. I'm far from a pro at relationships. I've lived with families as an outsider. You pointed that out. But I've seen the work needed to have a successful relationship. It's hard work. Often boring, not fun. That's part of what scares me. Good times aren't always guaranteed. Walking away isn't—shouldn't be—an option. At least not with me. I can't do that. You can't do that to me."

"I get that. I do. No pre nup, okay? My dad will understand. No walking away. We date, we marry then we live happily ever after through the good times, boring times and whatever else life brings."

She couldn't believe the words he was saying. "That's all I want. I'm finished keeping myself distanced. From the families I worked for, the animals I've fostered, even things I've purchased and where I've lived. I've kept my emotional liabilities and attachments to a minimum, but I don't want to do that anymore. Especially with you."

Hope filled his eyes. "Is that a yes?"

"Yes, I'm ready to take the leap, but only with you." The smile on her face grew by the second. "I'll give you another chance and another after that, but only if you'll do the same with me."

"I love you, Emma Markwell." AJ kissed her on the lips. "You can have as many chances as you want."

Something bumped against her leg. She looked down. "Blossom."

The cat purred.

Declan held on to the end of the cat's leash. "Only for you, bro. Only for you."

AJ laughed, then brushed his lips over Emma's again. "I'm going to like kissing you for real."

She nodded. "We're going to need a lot of practice."

"Wonderful, wonderful. My birthday wish came true!" Lilah hugged Emma, an embrace full of love, acceptance and rose-scented perfume. "Now all I need is for the rest of my unmarried grandchildren to find their true loves."

True love.

Emma sighed, resting her head against AJ's chest and feeling the beat of his heart against her cheek. That was what she'd found in Haley's Bay. True love and a family.

Blossom meowed.

Not to mention a cat.

"Well, don't look at us for help, Grandma," AJ teased. "We'll be too busy getting to know each other, then we'll need to talk about the future, wedding plans and where to honeymoon. But not until after we spend more time together and make things official."

Emma's heart overflowed with joy at the thought of getting married and being AJ's wife. She wanted to pinch herself to make sure she wasn't dreaming. Except none of her dreams had ever been this good.

"Not to worry." Lilah beamed. "These things have a way of working themselves out. Isn't that right, Blossom?"

As if on cue, Blossom meowed. The cat rubbed against AJ's leg, then head butted Emma's calf.

AJ rubbed the scruff of Blossom's neck. "Looks like our cat agrees with you, Grandma."

"I agree, too." Satisfaction filled Emma. She wiggled her toes. "Things do have a way of working out."

"When you least expect it," AJ said.

Emma's heart sighed. "I wouldn't have it any other way."

* * * * *

COMING NEXT MONTH FROM

HARLEQUIN®

SPECIAL EDITION

Available August 19, 2014

#2353 MAVERICK FOR HIRE
Montana Mavericks: 20 Years in the Saddle! • by Leanne Banks
Nick Pritchett has a love 'em and leave 'em attitude...except when it comes to his best friend, Cecelia Clifton. When the pretty brunette insists on finding a beau, the hunky carpenter realizes that he can't lose Cecelia to another man. Nick may be Mr. Fix-It in Rust Creek Falls, but his BFF has done a number on his heart!

#2354 WEARING THE RANCHER'S RING
Men of the West • by Stella Bagwell
Cowboy Clancy Calhoun always had room for only one woman in his heart—his ex-fiancée, Olivia Parsons, who left him years ago. So when Olivia returns home to Nevada for work, Clancy is blown away. But can the handsome rancher simultaneously heal his wounded heart *and* convince Olivia to start a life together at long last?

#2355 A MATCH MADE BY BABY
The Mommy Club • by Karen Rose Smith
Adam Preston never worried about babies...that is, until he had his sister's infant to care for! Bewildered at his new responsibilities, Adam asks pediatrician Kaitlyn Foster for help. The good doctor is reluctant to give her assistance, but once she does, she just can't resist the bachelor and his adorable niece.

#2356 NOT JUST A COWBOY
Texas Rescue • by Caro Carson
Texan oil heiress Patricia Cargill is particular when it comes to her men, but there's just something about Luke Waterson she can't resist. Maybe it's that he's a drop-dead gorgeous rescue fireman and ranch hand! Luke, who lights long-dormant fires in Patricia, has also got his fair share of secrets. Can the cowboy charm the socialite into a happily-ever-after?

#2357 ONCE UPON A BRIDE
by Helen Lacey
Although she owns a bridal shop, Lauren Jakowski can't imagine herself taking the trip down the aisle anytime soon. In fact, she's sworn off men for the foreseeable future! But Cupid intervenes in the form of her new next-door neighbor, Gabe Vitali. Despite his tragic past, the cancer survivor might just be the key to Lauren's future.

#2358 HIS TEXAS FOREVER FAMILY
by Amy Woods
After a difficult divorce, art teacher Liam Campbell wants nothing more than to start anew in Peach Leaf, Texas. He's instantly captivated by his new boss, Paige Graham, but the lovely widow has placed romance on the back burner to care for her emotionally wounded young son and focus on her career. Still, as Liam bonds with the boy and his mother, a new family begins to blossom.

YOU CAN FIND MORE INFORMATION ON UPCOMING HARLEQUIN® TITLES, FREE EXCERPTS AND MORE AT WWW.HARLEQUIN.COM.

HSECNM0814

REQUEST YOUR FREE BOOKS!

2 FREE NOVELS PLUS 2 FREE GIFTS!

♦ HARLEQUIN®

SPECIAL EDITION

Life, Love & Family

YES! Please send me 2 FREE Harlequin® Special Edition novels and my 2 FREE gifts (gifts are worth about $10). After receiving them, if I don't wish to receive any more books, I can return the shipping statement marked "cancel." If I don't cancel, I will receive 6 brand-new novels every month and be billed just $4.74 per book in the U.S. or $5.24 per book in Canada. That's a savings of at least 14% off the cover price! It's quite a bargain! Shipping and handling is just 50¢ per book in the U.S. and 75¢ per book in Canada.* I understand that accepting the 2 free books and gifts places me under no obligation to buy anything. I can always return a shipment and cancel at any time. Even if I never buy another book, the two free books and gifts are mine to keep forever.

235/335 HDN F45Y

Name	(PLEASE PRINT)

Address	Apt. #

City	State/Prov.	Zip/Postal Code

Signature (if under 18, a parent or guardian must sign)

Mail to the Harlequin® Reader Service:
IN U.S.A.: P.O. Box 1867, Buffalo, NY 14240-1867
IN CANADA: P.O. Box 609, Fort Erie, Ontario L2A 5X3

**Want to try two free books from another line?
Call 1-800-873-8635 or visit www.ReaderService.com.**

* Terms and prices subject to change without notice. Prices do not include applicable taxes. Sales tax applicable in N.Y. Canadian residents will be charged applicable taxes. Offer not valid in Quebec. This offer is limited to one order per household. Not valid for current subscribers to Harlequin Special Edition books. All orders subject to credit approval. Credit or debit balances in a customer's account(s) may be offset by any other outstanding balance owed by or to the customer. Please allow 4 to 6 weeks for delivery. Offer available while quantities last.

Your Privacy—The Harlequin® Reader Service is committed to protecting your privacy. Our Privacy Policy is available online at www.ReaderService.com or upon request from the Harlequin Reader Service.

We make a portion of our mailing list available to reputable third parties that offer products we believe may interest you. If you prefer that we not exchange your name with third parties, or if you wish to clarify or modify your communication preferences, please visit us at www.ReaderService.com/consumerchoice or write to us at Harlequin Reader Service Preference Service, P.O. Box 9062, Buffalo, NY 14269. Include your complete name and address.

Cecelia Clifton came to Rust Creek Falls hoping to find true love. Then she fell for Nick Pritchett, the commitment-phobic Thunder Canyon carpenter she's known all her life. But when Nick agrees to give his best friend boyfriend-catching lessons, he discovers that there's more to Cecelia than meets the eye—and that he wants her all for himself!

***

"I know these are for the charity auction, but if I give you twenty-five bucks, will you give me a bite of something?"

He must be desperate, Cecelia thought. Plus there was also the fact that she knew that Nick did a lot of charity work. He was always helping out people who couldn't pay him. Her heart softened a teensy bit. "Okay. Two apple muffins for twenty-five bucks. Frosting or not?"

"I'll take one naked," he said and shot her a naughty look. "The other frosted."

His sexy expression got under her skin, but she told herself to ignore it. She handed him a hot cupcake. "It's hot," she warned, but he'd already stuffed it into his mouth.

He opened his mouth and took short breaths.

She shook her head. "When will you learn? When?" she asked and frosted a cupcake, then set it in front of him. "Now that you've singed your taste buds," she said.

He walked to the fridge and grabbed a beer then gulped it down. "Now for the second," he said.

"Where's my twenty-five bucks?" she asked.

"You know I'm good for it," he said and pulled out his wallet. He extracted the cash and gave it to her. "There."

"Thank you very much," she said and put the cash in her pocket.

Within two moments, he'd scarfed down the second cupcake, then pulled a sad expression. "Are you sure you can't give me one more?"

"I'm sure," she said.

He sighed. "Hard woman," he said, shaking his head. "Hard, hard woman."

"One of my many charms," she said and smiled. "You always eat the baked goods I give you in two bites. Don't you know how to savor anything?"

He met her gaze for a long moment. His eyes became hooded and he gave her a smile that branded her from her head to her toes. "There's only one way for you to find out."

***

Enjoy this sneak peek from
MAVERICK FOR HIRE
by New York Times *bestselling author Leanne Banks,*
the newest installment in the brand-new six-book continuity
MONTANA MAVERICKS:
20 YEARS IN THE SADDLE!,
coming in September 2014!

HARLEQUIN®

SPECIAL EDITION

Life, Love and Family

Coming in September 2014

WEARING THE RANCHER'S RING

by *USA TODAY* bestselling author

Stella Bagwell

Cowboy Clancy Calhoun always had room for only one woman in his heart—his ex-fiancée, Olivia Parsons, who left him six years ago. So, when Olivia returns home to Nevada for work, Clancy is blown away. But can the handsome rancher simultaneously heal his wounded heart *and* convince Olivia to start a life together, at long last?

Don't miss the latest edition of the
***MEN OF THE WEST* miniseries!**

Enjoy **THE BABY TRUTH** *and*
ONE TALL, DUSTY COWBOY,
already available from the
MEN OF THE WEST *miniseries by Stella Bagwell.*

Available wherever books and ebooks are sold.

www.Harlequin.com

HSE65836

Love the Harlequin book you just read?

Your opinion matters.

Review this book on your favorite book site, review site, blog or your own social media properties and share your opinion with other readers!

Be sure to connect with us at:
Harlequin.com/Newsletters
Facebook.com/HarlequinBooks
Twitter.com/HarlequinBooks

HARLEQUIN®
A *Romance* FOR EVERY MOOD™

Stay up-to-date on all your
romance-reading news with the
Harlequin Shopping Guide,
featuring bestselling authors, exciting new
miniseries, books to watch and more!

The newest issue will be delivered right to you
with our compliments! There are 4 each year.

Signing up is easy.

EMAIL

ShoppingGuide@Harlequin.ca

WRITE TO US

HARLEQUIN BOOKS
Attention: Customer Service Department
P.O. Box 9057, Buffalo, NY 14269-9057

OR PHONE

1-800-873-8635 in the United States
1-888-343-9777 in Canada

Please allow 4-6 weeks for delivery of the first issue by mail.